SEEKING JUSTICE

THE COWBOY JUSTICE ASSOCIATION
BOOK ELEVEN

www.OliviaJaymes.com

Seeking Justice

Sometimes happily ever after isn't forever…

With Wade Bryson on the loose, Kaylee is pitching in to help her best friend Ava take care of the twins while they're in hiding. Unfortunately, that means being close to her estranged husband Reed. No one knows they've separated. Not wanting to burden her friends with her own issues, she's going to have to pretend to be the happy, loving wife.

Reed still loves Kaylee and just wants his wife back. For the last several months she's been a shadow of her former self and he's at a loss as to what to do. Their marriage is in shambles, Kaylee can barely look at him, and now they've been thrown together to help their friends evade a serial killer. All he wants is a second chance.

Their relationship has been tested to its limits and is teetering on the brink. It's going to take an extraordinary love to bring this couple back together.

CHAPTER ONE

R eed Mitchell wasn't having much luck making conversation with his wife Kaylee. Since picking her up, she'd barely spoken except when answering a direct question. If that's how she was going to be, he could deal with it.

"Have you told Ava?"

Still staring out of the car window, she shook her head. "No, I assumed she had bigger problems with Wade Bryson breaking out of prison. Did you tell Logan?"

"No, I figured the same as you."

A long silence. He ought to be used to it by now, but it still frustrated the hell out of him. How had they gotten to this point? Barely speaking to one another? Kaylee only tolerating his presence?

"I guess they'll figure it out eventually."

He didn't want anyone to know that they'd separated. Because he still had hope that it was only temporary and that they'd work it out. She couldn't stay like this forever. Could she?

"You don't have to do this," he said. "If no one knows that means we're going to have to share a room. Act like we don't hate each other."

That got her attention. Quickly she turned from the scenery outside the window and looked at him. Finally. If only her green eyes weren't so cold. He rarely saw true happiness in Kaylee anymore. It hadn't been there in a long time. It was probably his fault. He'd tried but nothing ever seemed to make any difference.

Reed knew that Kaylee blamed herself. He didn't know how to stop her.

"I don't hate you." Her voice was small, barely above a whisper. "I've never hated you."

"You're doing a hell of an impression then," he said grimly, his jaw painfully tight. "This isn't how you act around someone you like, honey."

He'd done it again. Upset her. Her cheeks were pale and her lips pressed together in a thin line. "I'm sorry you don't approve. I'll try to do better. I'll act like my life is rainbows and unicorns."

At one point it had been. They'd been happy and in love. Then they'd taken it for granted, wanting too much apparently. They'd been greedy and look where it got them. Almost strangers.

Sighing, his fingers gripped the steering wheel, the knuckles white. "That's not what I meant. I'm glad you're here. Ava needs the support of her friends right now. I just wanted to warn you that it won't be easy when we're in front of other people. That is, if you don't want to tell people that I've moved out."

"I'm not ready to talk about it."

She might never be ready. She sure as hell didn't want to talk about the gigantic elephant in the room. The whole reason they were having problems.

"You can tell me anything, honey."

Kaylee shook her head, tears glistening on her eyes. "I've tried. You don't understand."

Reed didn't want to argue again. They'd argued too many times and they never made any real progress. They were simply running laps at this point.

"I want to understand but you can't blame yourself–"

"I said I don't want to talk about it. It doesn't change anything."

No, it didn't change the issue at hand.

"It might change how you feel. I don't care about having a baby. It's not that important to me."

A silvery tear slid down her creamy cheek. Now Reed felt like a total asshole. He'd made her cry mentioning the one thing that she didn't want to talk about. She never wanted to talk about it again. She'd made that clear the day they'd walked out of that fertility specialist's office.

"You're lying. It was important. To both of us."

"Our marriage is more important than a baby. We could always adopt."

Scrubbing at her wet cheeks, she turned away again. "You just don't get it."

"And that shuts down the conversation, doesn't it?" Reed's voice had become louder and his heart beat faster in his chest. The ties that bound them together felt so fragile these days, as if they might snap at any moment. He was constantly reaching out to pull her closer but that just pushed her farther away. "Dumb old Reed doesn't get it so you stop talking. Stop believing in our marriage. It's all your way and I don't get any say."

"Nothing has been my way."

The words were barely audible, but Reed still heard them. Dammit, he loved this woman. He'd die for her without any question. But he couldn't make her happy. Shit, when was the last time he'd seen her smile? He couldn't remember. All the joy that had been inside of his wife had leaked out, leaving a shell of a human being. She existed but barely. She worked and some-times she'd eat. She rarely left the house and she hardly spoke to anyone especially him. It had been like living with a shadow. The day she'd asked him to leave he hadn't even argued. He'd packed his bag and left, mostly out of self-preservation.

Honestly, Reed needed to keep his head in the game and not be distracted by his own personal issues. He'd hoped when Kaylee had said she was coming to help out that the time together might give him a chance to heal his marriage, but they both had to want that. Right now, he was alone in wanting to make this work. The days to come weren't going to be easy. In fact, being this close to her and not pulling her into his arms was a particularly cruel form of torture. He still loved his wife desperately. Sometimes he thought she still loved him, too.

The safe house was located on the outskirts of Billings. Close enough to law enforcement but far enough away that they had some privacy. It was state of the art technologically and administered by the Marshal service. Their friend Evan Davis had once been a US Marshal, so he was the liaison with the service who was looking for Wade, but they were also helping protect Ava, Logan, and the kids.

They were all helping. Tanner, Seth, Griffin, Jared, Jason, and Dare. They were banded together now, a team. No one was going to get to Logan and his family.

No one. If only he could somehow protect his wife from the world.

"Are you happy, honey?"

"I don't know. Are you?"

"We could be. It doesn't have to be like this."

Reed pulled up to the front of the house and parked the car. In a few seconds, they would be onstage. They might not be a couple, but they had to act like it. Kaylee gathered her purse and backpack, pushing open the car door.

"The difference between the two of us, Reed, is that I don't expect to be happy."

If he couldn't get Kaylee back... Neither did he.

The safe house where Logan, Ava, and the kids were staying was lovely and spacious with soaring ceilings and shiny maple floors. It looked comfortable but a little cold and unlived in, more like a showroom than a home.

But Ava had a wide smile on her face and open arms which Kaylee flew into gratefully, hugging her best friend hard. It had been far too long since they'd seen each other in person. Skype sessions were fine, but they simply weren't the same. Already the tension that had built during the car ride was draining away.

"I've missed you," Ava gushed, giving Kaylee a second hug. "I'm so glad that you're here but you didn't have to come."

"I wanted to come. I thought you might need a hand with the twins, keeping them occupied."

Rolling her eyes, Ava gestured toward the back of the house. "Logan has them in the backyard right now and they're all getting dirty playing kickball. We're trying to keep them outside as much as possible to wear them out. So far it seems to be working."

"Do they know...?"

Ava shook her head. "They think we're on an extended vacation. They don't question having Uncle Reed or Uncle Tanner around. They're not too sure about the marshals but we just told them that they're family friends. If this goes on much longer, however, they're going to know something is up. They're getting older and far too smart to be fooled. Now that you're here I think we've bought at least a week. They didn't understand why Uncle Reed was here but Aunt Kaylee wasn't."

Kayla felt a pang in her heart at Ava's words. Reed was here but she hadn't been. A common state these days, although she wasn't sure she'd ever get used to it. The being alone part was painful.

"I'm here now," Kaylee replied, forcing a smile to her face. It was strange and uncomfortable but being here with Ava was the closest feeling to happiness that she'd had in a long time. "We'll come up with some great games. Are we allowed to leave the compound?"

There had been gates and a long driveway to the main house. On the way, they'd passed a guest house where Reed had said the marshals were staying.

"We can but we're trying not to, if you know what I mean. The two marshals have an opinion on just about everything we do and if it were up to them we'd be hunkered down in the house twenty-four seven with the curtains drawn. Luckily, we have the final say. Logan and I discussed this and then talked about it with Jared and we all agree that we can't keep the children prisoners in this house. Logan knows Wade the best and he doesn't think that he'd go after the twins."

"What about you?"

Shrugging as if she didn't care, Ava sniffed at the question. "He might regret that. I'm not inclined to go quietly, if you know what I mean."

Ava would put up a hell of a fight and Wade wouldn't know what hit him.

"Seriously," Ava's expression grew sober. "This is sort of dangerous. You didn't have to come, and I'd understand if you decided to go home."

Ava had no idea. The most dangerous thing about being here was being so close to Reed.

Clearing his throat, Reed made his presence known. Before he was happy to let the women have their reunion. "I told her that, Ava, but she was determined to come and support you."

"I trust that you're well protected," Kaylee said, keeping her gaze on her friend and not on her husband. She could feel him close though, the heat from his body radiating out. He'd always been like that – a walking heater. At night, she'd wake up covered in sweat because they'd cuddled, their legs and arms tangled together like two puppies. "I'm not worried about my safety."

Ava glanced over her shoulder. "You'll probably want to go upstairs and unpack. Then why don't you come outside and say hello to Logan and the twins? I can take you for a little tour of the place too and introduce you to the marshals."

"What are they like?"

Kaylee had visions of bossy people that were heavily armed. She'd watched far too many movies.

"Nice. Professional. They keep their distance for the most part, but they seem okay. It's their job to keep Wade off of the property. So far, so good. Assuming he's even coming for Logan. It's just a theory."

A decent one, though. It made sense and they were right to be cautious.

Reed picked up Kaylee's suitcase. "Are you ready? I can show you our room."

Our room. Our room. Our room.

The words flitted around her brain, almost making her dizzy. A huge part of her wanted to turn and run out of the house. She'd made a big mistake coming here and thinking she could do this. Another part of her wanted to be here for her best friend and a little voice in her ear assured her that she could indeed do this. She could spend time with Reed and it wouldn't be a bad thing.

Those little voices were full of shit.

That tension back in full force, Kaylee silently followed her estranged husband up a staircase and down a long hallway to what would be their bedroom. She hadn't shared a bed with Reed in months and this wasn't going to be easy. Every single second she wanted to throw herself into his arms and sob, beg him to tell her that everything was going to be okay.

Then she'd remind herself that nothing was the same anymore. She'd seen the look on his face when that doctor had told them that her chances of ever getting pregnant were slim to none. His pain and…yes, disappointment.

With her. He'd been disappointed in her. And from experience she knew what that meant. What had she said to Reed when they'd first met?

When the going gets tough, men get gone.

This was certainly the toughest thing that had ever happened to her.

Kaylee's body had let her down and she'd let her husband down. At that moment the frustration and self-loathing that had been building for so long had exploded. She'd turned to the man she loved for comfort and reassurance and found a cold shoulder to cry on. There had been no soft landing, no hugs and cuddles with sweet words of love and adoration. Reed had said no words on the way home, barely acknowledging her existence. Once in the house he'd disappeared into the garage and not come back out until dinner. He'd acted normally after that, but she couldn't forget his first reaction.

His *true* reaction.

Now she was here with him again and he said that he wanted to understand. She was just so tired of talking with him. They went over the same ground again and again and they didn't seem to get anywhere. He couldn't comprehend her devastation and he hadn't tried. He kept saying that she should be fine, but she didn't feel fine, and he didn't seem to have any patience for that.

Reed set her suitcase on the queen-sized bed. The bedroom was decorated in blue and grey with small touches of green. It had an impersonal air about it, no photos or clutter except for Reed's tennis shoes tucked beside a chair. He'd always been a stickler for neatness while she was rather more slapdash and casual.

"There's plenty of room in the closet and the dresser. I didn't bring all that much with me."

Reed could always be counted on to pack light. She, on the other hand, brought thirty outfits when six or seven would suffice. She used to think that their opposite habits were cute but now…

She wanted to be alone, if only for a few minutes. She need-ed to breathe, and she couldn't do it when Reed was standing next to her.

"I'll be down as soon as I finish unpacking and freshening up. It won't take long."

"I'll pour you a glass of iced tea. I think there's cookies too to tide you over until lunch."

Her stomach lurched at the thought of food. It was the last thing she wanted.

"Thank you."

Without another word, Reed turned on his heel and left the room, closing the door softly behind him. Kayla sank onto the mattress and buried her head in her hands, tears beginning to well in her eyes. Blinking several times, she forcefully held them back. She'd become adept at hiding her pain and she'd need that skill while she was here.

Because Reed reminded her of all that she wasn't and never would be.

CHAPTER TWO

Out in the backyard, Ava pulled Logan aside so that no one could hear their conversation. Reed was talking to the female marshal Amy Sinclair and the male marshal Mike Dayton was patrolling the edge of the large area. The twins were in their swimsuits kicking a ball and running through the sprinklers.

"Has Reed said anything to you?"

Logan's brows shot up. "About what?"

"About him and Kaylee. You could have cut the tension between them with a knife when they arrived a few minutes ago. She barely looked at him and he seemed extremely uncomfortable."

"They probably just had a spat in the car on the way here. You know how that is."

Ava did, of course. She and Logan didn't always see eye to eye and they both had strong personalities. But...she hadn't known Reed and Kaylee to argue very often. Kaylee was the very definition of laidback and mellow so she rarely lost her temper.

"It was more than a spat. It was almost like they didn't like each other."

Which was crazy. Kaylee and Reed were deeply in love.

They'd gone through hell to be together.

"Maybe she's a little hormonal or something."

There were moments – like now – that Ava wanted to slap her husband's forehead. Hard.

"Did you actually just suggest that she's PMSing? Seriously?"

Logan had the good sense to take a step back. "I'm suggesting that maybe she's not in a good mood and is tired. Maybe she should lie down or something. I am not suggesting that she's overreacting. I'm suggesting that *you're* overreacting. They're married, they're going to argue. That's just the way it is."

Shaking her head, Ava rubbed at her temples where a headache was blooming. "The stupidity of men never ceases to amaze me, and no, I'm not hormonal, either. Idiot."

"I never said I wasn't dumb."

Her husband had a goofy grin on his face. He was lucky he was so damn good-looking and sexy.

"I'm just worried."

"Did you ever think that you're worried about them, so you won't have to worry about our situation?"

Hmmm…that kind of made sense. "Since when did you become Sigmund Freud?"

Chuckling, Logan dropped a kiss on her nose. "Since I heard Reed say the same thing to me two days ago. I was ranting about…shit, I don't even remember now it was so fucking unimportant, but he said that perhaps I was upset because I didn't want to face my own situation. Shit, you can tell he's been in therapy."

"It's not a bad thing. Therapy can be quite helpful."

"I'm not saying it's not, but you can tell that he's been in it."

"I think you're full of bull."

"That's my beautiful wife, always supporting my ego and making me feel like Superman."

"As if you need any help," Ava snorted. "You have a king-sized ego and more than your share of self-esteem."

"That I do," he readily agreed. "But if you're so concerned I can try and get Reed to talk about it. There's nothing two men love more than talking about their feelings and shit."

Ava had a vision of Logan and all of his friends sitting around talking about how much they loved their wives and lamenting their gray hair and crow's feet.

"I think that might not be a good idea. I hope that you're right and I'm just overreacting."

While her friends were protecting her, she would be keeping an eye on them. Just in case.

With Kaylee upstairs and everyone else out in the backyard, Logan, Reed and Jared slipped into the office to call Tanner and catch up with what was going on with tracking Wade. The last thing they'd heard was that Wade had been spotted in a small town outside of Cheyenne driving a blue Honda Accord. Stolen, of course. He'd already dumped the original vehicle he'd escaped in forty-eight hours ago.

Logan sat behind the desk with Reed and Jared sitting in the leather chairs opposite. Tanner answered on the third ring.

"Marks."

There was no emotion in Tanner's voice, so Logan couldn't tell if he was happy, sad, or something completely different.

"Hey," Logan greeted his friend. "We were hoping to get an update. Is this a bad time?"

"Yes, but I can't think of a better one. We're in the process of regrouping and combing through the information that the tip line received."

Law enforcement officials had opened a tip line in hopes of

putting pressure on Wade. Personally, Logan thought the idea sucked. Wade didn't have the personality that would be bothered by a tip line and citizens keeping an eye out for him. If it did anything, it would make him more dangerous because he'd want lots of reports in the press.

"Anything worth following?"

"Lots of sightings but it's hard to know which are good and which are garbage," Tanner growled. "We have more information than we know what to do with. I think our best bet is a tip that Wade was seen in a black Chevy four-by-four about sixty miles from here. Our team is going to pursue that one. The other marshals will take different paths. We'll get the son of a bitch. The good news is that he's nowhere near you."

Yet.

"We can't relax," Logan warned. "He could have one or more groupies working for him. We know he has admirers who would love his attention."

"And that's why you have people all around. No one is going to get near you. Now I do have some other news. Dare had to return home. Both Rayne and Cherish came down with the stomach flu. Her sister is holding down the fort until he gets there but I told him to go home. We're going to have to do this without him."

"Dare's a good man and he'll be missed. I hope his family recovers quickly."

They chatted a little more and then Tanner had to get back on the road with Seth, Griffin, and Jason. Logan hung up and leaned forward, propping his elbows on the desk.

"So what do you think?"

Scratching his chin, Jared gave them a huge grin. "I think that I'm glad that we're here in this comfortable house and they're on the road drinking bad coffee and crammed into an

SUV twenty-four hours a day."

"I'll second that," Reed laughed. "They're taking turns sleeping and they're eating crappy food. At least we get to sleep in a bed at night."

"I know what you're thinking," Jared said, levering up from the chair. "You want to be out there on the road looking for Wade. That's a terrible idea and you know it."

"I could make a good argument for being out there," Logan replied. "I could help."

"You're helping from here," Reed said. "You're the one that knows how Wade thinks."

"And no one is listening to me," Logan snorted. "They set up that damn tip line even though I told them it was a bad idea. Wade won't hesitate to kill anyone that recognizes him, and he won't hesitate to kill to get his name in the news. He doesn't care about human life at this point. People are expendable to him."

"Do you think that includes Marilyn Bartlett?" Jared asked, checking out the window. "Is he capable of having any feelings for her?"

Marilyn Bartlett was the prison psychologist who had fallen under Wade's spell and had helped him break out of prison. She'd even killed for him and was now on the run as well which left her at the mercy of Wade.

And he didn't have any mercy.

"No," Logan said bluntly. "She's safe as long as he has a use for her. When he's done... Well, let's just say I hope she sees the writing on the wall soon and gets out of there. He would never think she'd leave him, so he wouldn't put any safeguards around her. She could slip away at any time."

Reed seemed to ponder his words. "But he would stop her if he caught her."

"He'd kill her without a second thought," Logan said grimly.

"Not one regret. He doesn't care. He might have at one point but he's long past that now."

Reed tapped the oak desk. "The best place for you is right here with your family."

Restlessly, Logan stood and stretched. He'd been cooped up for far too long. He was used to being a hell of a lot more active. "I thought at the forty-eight hour mark we'd have him. I didn't think it would go on this long. We all know that with every passing hour the chances of catching Wade grow smaller and smaller. Most fugitives are brought in quickly."

"As you've pointed out, Wade isn't your average prison escapee," Jared said. "He's smart and devious as hell. He'll do whatever it takes to evade capture."

Logan shook his head, his jaw tight with tension. "You know what the funny thing is? Way back I would have told you that Wade was just a soft, spoiled businessman that didn't know shit about life. I could never have imagined…this. He didn't seem like the type."

"He's evolved," Reed said. "Quickly. When he was killing before it changed him fundamentally, and then he escalated even more when he was inside. He learned what he needed to know."

"I believe that he's been preparing for this since the day he was arrested."

Reed nodded. "I think you're right. The fucker's patient, I'll give him that. We have to be even smarter and more patient. It's been forty-eight hours but that's nothing to Wade. Has he contacted you yet?"

Logan pulled his phone from his pocket. "No, but my gut says that he will. He'll want the attention and he's definitely going to want to taunt me. Let me know that I haven't caught him. He'll probably also throw in a threat or two to my family. He wants to spook me, get me off my game."

"We're not going to let him do that," Jared said, his arms crossed over his chest and his expression serious. "Fuck him and his mind games. No one is going to get near this house."

"If he can't get me here, he'll do something else for the attention. If he stops being the number one story on the news that's just going to piss him off. He needs to be the center of it all. He needs to be the star. If he thinks that he's not, he's going to kill someone. Maybe several someones, assuming he hasn't already. He'd want the public scared. It would make him feel powerful."

"There might be a body out there that we haven't found," Reed said.

Logan shook his head. "He'd want us to find the body sooner rather than later. He'd put it right in our path. Remember, the show is important. He'd want us to know what he'd done, and the theatrics are as much fun for him as the actual act of murder."

Maybe more. Wade got off on notoriety. He'd developed a taste for it and he wasn't going to stop and lay low until the heat was off. He was smart, but he was also ruled by his compulsions and that made him foolhardy. Eventually he was going to do something stupid. Then they'd have him.

The stupidest thing Wade could do is come after Logan but that was exactly what he was going to do. It was only a matter of time.

I'll be ready.

CHAPTER THREE

Kaylee picked up a few of the scattered toys in the living room and placed them on the empty bookshelves. Logan was upstairs with the twins giving them their bath while she and Ava fixed their bedtime snack and straightened up after an active day.

"I can read them their stories tonight if you want me to," Kaylee offered, placing the last toy truck away. She didn't want some poor unsuspecting person to patrol the house in the middle of the night and break their ankle.

"They'd love that," Ava replied, placing a few apples slices onto a plate along with some cubes of cheese. "They're always talking about their Aunt Kaylee. You do the voices when you read the book, so they think you're amazing, which of course you are. And not just because you do *The Three Little Pigs*."

"I'll huff and I'll puff and I'll blow your house down," Kaylee recited, making her voice as low and growly as she could. She was playing the wolf, after all. "It's fun to read to them."

"It is, although I have to admit I'm going to enjoy the break tonight," Ava laughed. "I'll let you decide if they get just *one more* story or not."

A lump formed in Kaylee's throat and tears pricked the backs of her eyes at the thought of holding a child in her arms. He or she would look up at her with their big hazel eyes – just like Reed's – and beg for another story. Or a drink of water. Anything so that they didn't have to go to bed. Then she'd get to hold them a little while longer.

But her arms were empty.

"I'm happy to read to them," Kaylee said through her tight throat. "They're so cute and well-behaved."

"They are," Ava agreed. "But they have their moments like any child."

"You're good parents."

"We try but it isn't easy." Ava paused, and Kaylee knew what was coming next. There had been a question in the air all day. "Is everything okay between you and Reed? I sensed some tension when you arrived, and you've barely been in the same room. Logan said you two probably just had a tiff in the car and he's probably right, but you know you can talk to me? About anything."

Kaylee wanted to talk to Ava. Truly, she did, but... It was too hard and painful. She didn't want to see the sympathy in her friend's eyes. She didn't want anyone's pity.

"We are sort of arguing," Kaylee finally said. It wasn't a lie. These days they couldn't agree on the color of the sky. "But I'm sure we'll work it out. I appreciate the concern, though."

"If you want to talk about it–"

"I don't," Kaylee replied quickly, cutting off Ava. She couldn't think of a subject she wanted to discuss less. "I really don't."

Her friend looked of two minds about responding but she nodded and smiled. "Just know that I'm here for you. Looks like the twins are ready for their snack and story."

Logan and Reed were coming down the stairs along with Brianna and Colt, both sparkling clean and in their pajamas. Brianna's long hair was still damp and curling at the ends just like her mother's. Every time Kaylee saw the children they seemed to look more like their parents.

I can do this. I can get through this.

Taking a deep breath despite her tight chest, Kaylee gave the children a dazzling grin and held out her arms for hugs. Brianna was the first to throw herself into her aunt's arms and Kaylee breathed in deeply of that childhood scent – a mix of baby shampoo and fabric softener. Colt was next, and he giggled when Kaylee tickled his ribs, smacking a kiss against her cheek. Her chest closed around her heart making it difficult to breathe.

Ignoring her internal tumult, she held up a couple of books. "How about this one? Or do you want the one with the dinosaurs?"

"Dinosaurs!" Colt yelled at the top of his lungs, causing the adults to wince. "I want dinosaurs!"

"Colt," Ava said in a warning tone. "It's Brianna's turn to pick a story."

"The princess one first," said the little girl. "Then the dinosaur."

To his credit, Colt gave in easily and the three of them cuddled on the couch, one on either side of Kaylee, leaning their sleepy heads on her arms. The others sat down as well, Logan and Ava on the loveseat and Reed on the armchair not that far away. His gaze was laser focused on Kaylee, making it difficult to do anything let alone read and animate a story, but somehow she managed to do it. The entire time they sat there he didn't pull his eyes away from her, his expression inscrutable.

She didn't have to ask what he was thinking. She already knew. He was thinking about how much he'd like to have his own children. He wanted to read to them before bed and help with their bath. He wanted to carry them up to bed on his shoulders and then kiss them goodnight. He wanted to check closets for monsters and under the bed for the boogeyman.

If he stayed with Kaylee, he wasn't going to get to do any of that. He said he didn't care but at moments like this… He showed just how much he did.

If someone took Kaylee's blood pressure right now it would break the machine. After thirty minutes of torture downstairs reading to Brianna and Colt, she wasn't even close to finding any peace and serenity. She and Reed were sharing a room and a bed, something they hadn't done in months.

She'd hated her empty bed at home after he'd moved out, but she wasn't ready to have him back in it, either. Growing used to it again was a recipe for disaster. She was supposed to be learning to live without him, but all she was finding out was that a world without Reed in it was gray and lifeless.

Barely able to look at herself in the bathroom mirror, she tried to avoid her reflection but it seemed to mock her every movement. When she brushed her teeth, when she washed her face, when she combed her hair. It was always there even when she was home. Maybe if only to remind her that she still existed and hadn't faded away like a ghost.

She'd put on weight in the last few years courtesy of all the hormones she'd been on. Pinching the muffin top around her waist it didn't disappear when she scowled at it, stubbornly staying put. The doctor had assured her that the gain would only be temporary and that she would go back to the way she'd been before.

Those had been his exact words. Except that she wasn't. She

was changed forever only no one seemed to see it.

Those hormones. They'd played havoc with her body and emotions. Reed would come home to find her crying at commercials or screaming angry at some imagined slight. He'd been understanding and patient at first, but then less as time went on and her emotions spiraled further out of control. He'd started spending more evenings at work and less at home, leaving her alone with her thoughts far too often. She didn't blame him. If she could have stepped out of her body and left she would have done it, too.

Then there had been the nausea, the bloating, and the terrible headaches. And she'd done it gladly because it meant there was a chance. A small one, but she'd had hope.

The hope was gone and now she had to figure out how to live her life. She had many years ahead of her and she couldn't keep going on like this. Something had to change. But how? She was just so damn tired every day she could barely get out of bed. She'd grabbed at this chance to help out Ava and Logan because it gave her days purpose and she desperately needed that.

Gathering all the scraps of courage she had, Kaylee pulled open the bathroom door and entered the attached bedroom. Reed was lounging on the bed watching the television on the wall, the remote in his hand. The sight made her smile, remembering how when they'd first got together she'd had to get used to how he liked to have control of the remote. She could have the thermostat, but he had to have the remote. If she wanted to make him antsy, all she had to do was hold it and flip aimlessly through the channels. It drove him crazy. Luckily, she wasn't picky about what she watched most of the time.

"Anything good on?"

She congratulated herself on sounding so normal as if this was the most natural thing in the world, sleeping in the same bed with her husband.

"Not really. I was going to watch the news but–"

"That's fine. I'm going to read."

Or try to. Retrieving her e-reader from her bag, she settled on the bed trying to put as much distance between them as she could on the queen-sized mattress. It wasn't much, as Reed was a big man with wide shoulders. He easily took up more than half of the space, especially the way he was sprawled out with the wingspan of a Boeing 747.

Barely able to concentrate on the words in front of her, Kaylee was far more aware of the man lying beside her. Every move of his fingers fascinated her, keeping her attention on him and not the blurred page. She remembered vividly the last time they'd made love. No, they'd had sex. They'd stopped making love a long time ago. Eventually sex had become the thing they did when the calendar told them to. All the fun creative games that they'd played had gone by the wayside and lovemaking had become serious business.

"Kaylee…are you listening to me?"

No, she hadn't been. She'd been far away during happier times.

"Sorry, I think I was dozing off."

She was as far from sleep as she could be, but he didn't need to know that.

"I was saying that Ava seems so happy that you're here. I'm glad you decided to come. I know that this isn't easy. For either of us."

It was damn hard but worth it. This was for her best friend in the world.

"There isn't anything I wouldn't do for Ava."

"Even be with me."

His tone was bitter, and she supposed he had a right to feel that way.

"I don't want to argue with you tonight."

"I don't want to argue with you either."

"Then why the little dig? You were trying to get a reaction from me."

He sat up and placed the remote on the nightstand. "Maybe I was. Jesus, you're like a fucking zombie, Kaylee. Show an emotion. Any fucking emotion. Even if it's just that you hate my guts."

"I told you that I don't hate you."

"And yet, you don't want to be here with me. You don't want to be married to me. Just so we're clear, I want to be married to you. I want this time together to show you that I'm still your husband and I still love you. I think that you still love me."

She did. More than she knew how to express.

"Love has never been the problem."

He made a growling noise from deep in his chest. "I love you, Kaylee. Stop pulling away from me. We can get through this together."

At one time she'd agreed with that statement. She'd believed it with all of her heart and even depended on it. Now she knew the truth. Perhaps it was time to let him know that she did.

"I saw you that day."

His brows pinched together. "What day? I don't understand."

"The day the doctor told us that there was no hope for me to conceive. I saw your face that day. Your words said one thing, but your expression didn't lie. You thought I was a failure. You really aren't okay with not having children. You keep saying it, Reed, but deep inside I don't think you believe it."

Scraping his fingers through his short, dark hair, Reed swore softly under his breath. "As God as my witness, honey, I don't care. I really don't."

"I don't believe you," Kaylee replied softly. "I saw you that day. You pulled away from me and went off on your own. You'd always talk about how we would get through this together but when it all ended you just…left me all alone. That's when I needed you the most, Reed. You went off and I know why. You just don't want to admit that you're disappointed. You think it makes you look like a bad person. You're not. You're just human."

Opening and closing his mouth several times, her husband appeared to be trying to speak but no words would come out. His face was red, and his hazel eyes had turned an icy grey. He was angry and frustrated.

Throwing back the covers, Reed jumped out of bed and dragged on a pair of blue jeans as he hopped to the bedroom door. She'd expected him to slam it on his way out but he didn't, possibly out of deference to the others in the house. She could hear his footsteps down the hall, but they faded away until there was nothing but silence.

Then…and only then…did she allow the hot tears to flow.

CHAPTER FOUR

With a head full of steam, Reed stomped downstairs and into the kitchen for a beer. Normally he wouldn't drink but he wasn't on guard duty tonight and frankly, he needed the alcohol. What he really wanted was a double whiskey but that was out of the question.

The maple wood floors were cold under his bare feet. He should have stopped to put on a pair of socks, but he'd been so damn mad he could barely think straight. Did the woman that he loved actually believe that having a baby was more important to him than she was? It appeared that she did.

He didn't remember any abandoning going on, either.

Sure, he'd gone off by himself for a little while to lick his wounds. He'd be lying if he didn't admit that he'd been caught off guard by the news and he'd been justifiably upset. The doctor had been so calm and reassuring up to that point, although with each subsequent visit the news had become grimmer and grimmer. It was only human to be depressed when you'd wanted something so badly and found out it was never going to happen. He hadn't left her. He'd been there. He was sure of it.

He had to wonder, however, if he was pretending not to care? Was he in deep denial? Was Kaylee seeing something inside of him that he didn't know about himself? That couldn't be the case. He wasn't the most introspective guy, but he'd know if he resented his wife for not being able to get pregnant.

And what kind of guy would be like that? An asshole.

I am not an asshole. I'm a good husband.

But he was well aware that when he'd met Kaylee she hadn't been able to trust him at all. It had taken a huge leap of faith for her to believe in him and his love. He'd thought after all this time together she'd be past all of that, but just when he thought something was dead and buried it popped up out of the grave again. She hadn't had much luck with men staying when things weren't good. Now she believed he wanted out because everything wasn't perfect. He didn't know how to convince her that she was wrong.

Twisting the cap off of the beer bottle, he tossed it into the trash can and sat down at the table near the window. Mike and Jared were out there tonight, watching the perimeter while Amy took up guard inside. Reed would take his turn tomorrow. That's why he was here. To keep Ava, Logan, and the kids safe. Not to repair his wounded marriage. That had been a hope but not a very realistic one. They both had to want it and clearly Kaylee didn't.

"Can't sleep?"

Looking up from his beer, Reed was startled to see Amy standing in the kitchen doorway. She was probably just making the rounds and checking in with Mike to see if everything was okay.

"I've got a lot on my mind. Thought a beer might help me fall asleep."

"Want to talk about it?"

Amy retrieved a bottle of water from the refrigerator. She was an attractive woman around her early to mid-thirties with short dark hair and big brown eyes. Tall and slim, she was in excellent shape due to the physical demands of her job. The muscles in her arms were clearly displayed by the short sleeves of her t-shirt. She gave off an air of efficiency and capability.

But he wasn't going to spill his guts to a stranger.

"Not particularly."

She shrugged and sat down opposite him at the table. "That's fine. I was just being polite anyway. You don't really strike me as the 'let's talk about our feelings' kind of guy."

"I'm not."

"Okay, we'll talk about something else because I get bored when I have to stay up all night. How about football? Or baseball? Do you like sports?"

Taking another deep draw from the bottle, Reed took the time to study the woman sitting across from him. A dedicated agent and everyone seemed to like her. She knew her job and didn't have to be babysat by any of them.

It had been a long time. He wasn't getting any damn younger and he was rarely in situations alone with an attractive woman. Searching his brain, he couldn't remember the last time and warning bells were going off in his head.

Drink your beer and get out of here. Nothing good can come from this.

"No, I don't like sports."

It was a lie, but it seemed like a good idea not to encourage this any further. Even if she was only being nice.

"Are you one of those video game types?"

His marriage might be in shambles, but he wasn't looking for a replacement. Or a fling. Amy probably wasn't either, but he wasn't one to tempt fate.

"Work."

"You look like the dedicated type. I bet you're a workaholic." Amy looked up at the ceiling. "Does your wife not like it when you work so much? Anyone outside of law enforcement just doesn't understand."

"That's a personal question."

Kaylee had always been supportive of the time he'd spent at work. She was dedicated to her own job, too.

"I'm sorry. You seem unhappy. It's none of my business. I was just trying to help."

At one point, Reed would have said that the woman upstairs understood him better than he knew himself. She'd given him the time and space to figure out his life and now he wanted to return the favor. He simply hadn't known how hard it would be.

"I'm fine."

Her chair scraping loudly against the ceramic tile, Amy stood and screwed the lid on her water bottle. "I'm going to make the rounds. If you want to talk, I'm here."

His gaze swept her from head to toes. She didn't seem to be anything but nice.

"I won't but thanks."

"That's fine. Good night."

Amy left the kitchen and he drank down the last of the beer, tossing it in the trash as he stood. It was time to get out of here. The bedroom might be frosty and cold but down here was worse in a far different way.

How do I make her see that I love her?

Logan wasn't asleep when he heard the soft knock on his bedroom door. He'd barely slept since Tanner and all of his other sheriff friends had come to get them from the house in Corville and placed them into protective custody. He wasn't worried about their safety. Not much, anyway. He trusted his friends with his life. No, it was his brain that was the problem. His mind was far too active to allow restful sleep. Constantly thinking about what Wade was going to do next and where he might be. Catching him sooner rather than later would be best. Wade didn't care who he hurt and would surely wage a path of destruction a mile wide until he was safely behind bars again.

Ava must not have been sleeping well either because she sighed and levered up from the mattress slightly, pushing her long hair out of her face. "Someone's at the door."

"I know. Go back to sleep."

She was already shaking her head no. So stubborn. "It could be the kids."

"The kids wouldn't bother to knock, babe. Go back to sleep."

Of course, she didn't listen worth a damn. She tugged on her robe while he strode to the door, pulling it open a crack to see who was on the other side.

Jared, wearing a fucking grim expression on his face. Wade had done something and it wasn't good. Hopefully not too many innocent people had been hurt.

"I knew you'd want to know right away," Jared said. "Tanner and Seth found the vehicle that was thought to be stolen by Wade. Marilyn was in the trunk. Dead. Shot in the head."

Fuck, fuck, fuck.

Marilyn wasn't completely innocent, but she hadn't deserved this. It was a lesson though in that if you run with danger and evil it just might bite back at you. Logan had had a bad feeling all along about what Wade would do with Marilyn when she wasn't useful anymore. He wished he'd been wrong. He'd wanted to find Marilyn alive for many reasons, not the least of which was to hear what all she knew about Wade's plan once he'd broken out of prison.

Turning to where Ava stood behind him, he dropped a kiss on her forehead. "Go back to bed. I'm going downstairs to talk to Tanner and look at those maps again. Maybe I'll see something I didn't see before."

His beautiful but sleepy wife pointed to the clock on the bedside table. "It's almost five in the morning. I might as well get up and start some breakfast. I'm guessing that everyone but Kaylee and the kids are awake because of this news."

"I haven't woken Reed yet, but he was my next stop," Jared replied. "But yes, we're awake. I can make breakfast, though. It's no big deal."

"I seriously doubt I could go back to sleep after that morbid news," Ava said crisply. "I'll head downstairs and start the coffee. Sounds like it needs to be strong."

Ava headed downstairs while Logan and Jared woke Reed. They'd tried to be quiet but of course Kaylee woke up as well. Just like Ava, she insisted on going downstairs to help cook breakfast. The three men headed straight to the office where Mike and Amy had Tanner, Seth, and Evan Davis on the phone. Evan sounded surprisingly chipper but then Logan realized it was two hours later in Florida.

"If you're worried, we can bring everyone down here," Logan heard Evan say as they entered the room. "Wade can't get on a plane and it would take him a few days to travel here. No way could he head here and not be noticed."

"Hey Evan," Logan greeted the marshal-turned-sheriff-turned thriller novelist. "I appreciate the offer but we're trying not to venture too far from home in case I'm needed here for the manhunt. But I'm going to think about sending Ava and the kids down there. That might be a good idea."

"They'd never leave," Reed said. "You'd have to drug Ava

and tie her up to get her to go."

"True, but I'm not above doing that if I think she'll be safer. She's stubborn as a mule but if she thinks the kids will be better protected down there then she'll go. I'll talk to her about it."

"Whatever you decide is fine with me," Evan said. "You're always welcome here, whether it be just Ava and the twins or all four of you along with your protective detail. We also have several retired marshals in this area that would be glad to lend a hand as well. They're bored as shit."

"Is Tanner on the phone, too?" Logan asked.

"I am. Seth's also here."

"I'm not sure what you've already reported–"

"Not much," Tanner interrupted. "I was saving the details for you, if you're ready."

Jared was recording the call to ensure they didn't miss any information.

"Go ahead. We're all here."

"We got a tip through the phone line that Bryson was spotted at a drive-in restaurant about ten last night thirty miles from Cheyenne. That was in the opposite direction that we were traveling so we had to turn around. By the time we got to the area we drove down a two-lane side road that we thought would be a good route for Bryson. It was also near the drive-in he'd been seen at. We found the vehicle abandoned on the side of the road. Marilyn was in the trunk. One tap to the temple. I doubt she saw it coming."

Logan doubted that as well. Marilyn had trusted Wade for some God only knows reason. It had cost the psychiatrist her life.

"Any indication as to what direction he's headed or his mode of transport?"

"We're checking out the stolen car reports in this area.

There's one that looks the most promising. A 2015 Chevy Tahoe truck. Black. We just talked to the owner and he said that he'd darkened the windows which would be just what Bryson would want."

"Hardly low profile," Reed murmured. "A vehicle like that is going to call attention to itself."

"And that's what Wade wants," Logan said. "He's just getting started. Frankly, I'm shocked it's taken him this long to kill Marilyn. I predict very bad things happening from here and the time in between will get shorter and shorter."

"Agreed," Jared replied, that grim expression back in place. "Wade Bryson is like a ticking time bomb, and he's definitely going to explode. Have you been in touch with Jason's team?"

"We have," Tanner confirmed. "They're making a turn and heading toward us. From here we'll split up, taking two of the most likely paths. Logan, I don't suppose you have any wisdom there? Is there anywhere in this area that Wade would want to go to? Any place that he might know someone or feel safe?"

Logan had been asking himself that question since this whole fucking mess began. "I'm going to go back to the maps and try again. Nothing comes to mind right now but I'm not going to give up. There has to be something I'm missing. One thing I do know is that he has to have more help than we knew about. He wouldn't have killed Marilyn until he had someone else. Maybe he picked up someone right after. It would have to be someone he trusted and that means they're probably not on the right side of the law."

"We can help with that," Amy said, speaking for the first time in the conversation. Mike wasn't much of a talker, but Amy usually didn't hold back. "We'll use our database and find any ex-cons from the prison who live in that area."

"Also check for people who worked at the prison," Logan

instructed. "We've seen that he has power over people and can convince them to do things that they might not normally do."

"You act like he has some sort of freaky mind control," Mike laughed. "He's just a man."

"A man that convinced a woman who had never even had a traffic ticket to kill for him," Logan said, his teeth snapping together in frustration. This should have been over by now. He should be back in Seattle with his family enjoying the summer. "Don't underestimate Wade Bryson. I did, and he almost killed me. He doesn't have any conscience. We're like insects to him, only to be squashed when we get in the way. And eventually he's not even going to care who is a threat to him. He'll start killing because he enjoys it. He gets off on it."

"You sound very sure," Amy said. "We can only hope that you're not right. We don't need any other casualties in this situation."

Situation was a piss-poor way to describe the clusterfuck that they were smack dab in the middle of right now. Innocent people were almost certainly going to be hurt or killed.

"I hope that I'm wrong, but I don't think that I am. Wade's selection of vehicle tells me that he wants attention and to show off a little. That's not good news."

"So what's our next move?" Tanner asked. "We're going to follow our gut unless you tell us otherwise."

"For now, continue. I'll keep looking and researching. Let's talk again in about three hours."

That's what Logan's world had come down to. Three-hour increments and a fucking sociopath on the loose.

CHAPTER FIVE

Clearing the breakfast dishes from the long dining room table, Kaylee stopped and watched as Amy and Reed talked. They were about ten feet away so she couldn't hear what they were saying but their heads were close, almost…intimate. Amy's hand was on Reed's arm and Kaylee wanted to rip those fingers from her husband's skin.

A red-hot jealousy had come over Kaylee this morning. Amy and Reed had spent most of the morning meal talking and laughing with one another. Her husband had barely looked in Kaylee's direction which should have made her happy, but instead it pissed her off. The female marshal was all that Kaylee would never be. Tall and in great shape while Kaylee was short and soft. Sitting and writing books all day didn't lend itself to being a hardbody. Add in the weight she'd gained over the last few years… It was no wonder Reed seemed to be enjoying the attention of a beautiful woman. He hadn't had it at home. Not for a long time.

"If your eyes were lasers they would have bored a hole in Amy," Ava said in a soft whisper, coming to stand next to Kaylee. "You know he doesn't give a shit about her, right? He's just being polite."

Kaylee wanted to believe that but being polite didn't mean that you had to let other women touch you. That bitch's hand was still on Reed's arm and she was looking up at him like...

Dammit. This was what was going to happen when she separated officially from Reed. He was going to find another woman, a better woman, and Kaylee was going to live the rest of her life alone except for maybe the cats she was thinking about collecting. She'd better get used to this because Reed wasn't going to spend the second half of his life pining for her. He'd get on with it and find someone to share it with.

Someone else, that is. As in, not her.

Isn't this what you wanted?

That little voice inside of her had a taunting tone that set Kaylee's teeth on edge. This was what she'd wanted and she'd known it would hurt. She simply hadn't known how much until now.

It was physically painful as if she'd been shot and then stabbed in the heart, the knife twisted slowly around and around until she begged for mercy.

You pushed him away. He's only doing what you told him to.
I know that. I want him to be happy. It just hurts so much.

"Sure, he's just being polite."

"I'm going to make that offer again and say that if you want to talk I'm here for you."

Did she want to talk? Not talking wasn't helping much. She didn't want pity, but a sympathetic ear would be nice. She'd visited one of those support groups once, but she hadn't ever gone back. She hadn't been ready to talk about it with strangers, even ones that had walked in her shoes.

"I think...that I do want to talk," Kaylee finally said. "But not here. Somewhere we won't be interrupted or overheard."

If Ava was surprised that Kaylee had given in she didn't show it. She knew her friend so well she'd probably expected it. "Let me talk to Logan about watching the kids for a few minutes and then you and I can go up to my room. We won't be bothered there. We'll talk it all out and everything will be okay."

Ava didn't understand. Nothing was ever going to be the same.

"Reed and I separated about four months ago."

Kaylee and Ava were sitting in the latter's bedroom, both cross-legged on the bed, coffee in hand. The men and the children were downstairs and would hopefully stay there for at least a few minutes while she poured her heart out to her best friend in the whole world. She'd decided to just say it. Get it out there. She'd underestimated how much it would hurt to hear the words come out of her own mouth.

Eyes round and her mouth in the shape of an "O", Ava was horrified. "What? Separated? How come I didn't know this before now? Shit, forget that. Why? What happened? Did...did he...cheat?"

"I wish," Kaylee groaned. "Then I could just blame him. No, this is all my fault."

If anything, Ava's eyes grew even wider. "Did...did you cheat?"

The last word was said in a hushed whisper as if anyone would overhear.

"Of course not. No way would I ever cheat on Reed. I love him."

"But you're separated? Because you love him? Help a girl here. I'm not following this."

That tightness in Kaylee's chest was back, like a giant iron band around her heart growing ever smaller. Taking a deep breath, she plunged into the icy water and spoke her truth. She hadn't said it aloud to anyone. Not one person. Until now.

The truth will set you free.

Bullshit. It just makes me hurt.

"I can't have any children."

"I see."

Kaylee shook her head. "I doubt it. I can't have any children. Not ever. We've tried. Over and over. We've had all the tests. Fertility drugs. Assisted insemination. Nothing. The specialist – the third one I'd seen – finally told us that he didn't think he could do any more for us. He doubted that I could ever get pregnant. I have what is known as Unexplained Infertility."

"Unexplained infertility," Ava repeated. "You mean they don't know why?"

"They're not sure. There are many causes including egg quantity and quality. Or it could be endometriosis or perhaps a previous infection, although I don't remember any."

"So what happens now?"

"Nothing. There really isn't any more hope."

That was the hardest part. No hope.

"Nonsense," Ava's voice was firm. "There's always hope. You can find another doctor–"

"Stop," Kaylee commanded, placing her hand on Ava's. "Don't do this. I've spent the last three and a half years doing exactly that to myself and I'm exhausted. Worn out. I've seen multiple doctors and eventually they all say the same thing. It's not going to happen for me and that's what I've had to wrap my mind around. It's just not going to happen."

Just like herself though, Ava wasn't going to give up easily.

"There have to be treatments–"

"For what? There are treatments but for known causes. I

don't have a cause. Believe me when I say that I've done it all. The painful testing and the awful drugs. The side effects that were almost debilitating. I could barely write or function. And then add in the mood swings and I practically drove Reed away. I could be laughing one minute and crying the next. Some people have no side effects, some people have a few. Well, I had them all and even invented a few new ones. Suffice it to say I wasn't a good candidate." Kaylee sighed and rubbed at her temple which had begun to throb. "I know you're trying to help and you're the best friend I have, Ava. But believe me when I say that I can't keep my hope up anymore. You have no idea what it was like month after month to fail. I'd get my period and I'd just sit down and cry. Then I'd have to tell Reed and my God…his expression of disappointment each time. It was horrible. I never want to have to do that again. Ever."

There were tears in Ava's eyes. "I can't believe you were going through all of this and I never knew. I mean…I've seen you in person and I couldn't tell. Why didn't you talk to me?"

"Because I was ashamed."

There it was. The absolute truth of the matter.

"I was ashamed," Kaylee said again, needing to voice the emotion she'd felt for so long. "Women have babies. That's what we do. It's not all we do but it's not supposed to be this hard. At least I didn't think it would be. My body failed me."

That's when her own tears started, slowly at first and then a deluge that nothing could stop. Ava sat there with Kaylee as she sobbed, holding her and telling her that it was all going to be okay.

I want to believe that.

When the deluge finally subsided, Ava grabbed a box of tissues from the nightstand. "You have absolutely nothing to be ashamed of. So you can't have a baby. It doesn't make you less of a woman or anything, so don't even let your mind go there."

Ripping a tissue from the box, Kaylee dabbed at her wet cheeks. "Consciously I know that. But my subconscious…that fucker won't give me any rest. There's a little voice inside of me that keeps saying that I'm a failure. That I've let my husband down. How can he love me when I can't even give him a child? He wants to be a father so badly, Ava."

"I bet he wants to be your husband even more. Dear God, have you talked to Reed about this? Told him how you feel? He'd tell you that he loves you no matter what. I know that for a fact."

"I tried to tell him but he honestly doesn't want to hear it or acknowledge it. He keeps interrupting me and telling me I'm being overemotional. That it's the hormones that are making me feel this way. That I'll be better soon. But I saw his face that day, Ava. I saw how devastated he was. He pulled away when we should have been dealing with it together. And do you know why he pulled away? Because I'm the reason. Me. I'm the reason he can't be a father. I think he resents me but he doesn't want to admit it. That would make him a bad person."

Ava blew her red nose and then tossed the tissue into the small trashcan beside the bed. "Okay, you need to listen to me. I mean it. Listen to me. First of all, I bet the hormones have done a real number on you. I don't know how long they take to filter out of your system but they could have set you on this path and now you don't know how to change direction. Secondly, don't you think you should cut Reed some damn slack? He was upset and disappointed. He went off and licked his wounds privately. Men get like that sometimes. It doesn't mean he doesn't love you or resents you. That's the fertility drugs talking and you've bought into their shit hook, line, and sinker. He was shocked and he needed time to grieve. Have you grieved yet? I mean, really grieved."

Kaylee shook her head. "I don't know what you mean. We didn't lose a baby. I'm infertile."

"Yes, my friend, you did lose a baby." Ava placed her hands on either side of Kaylee's face so she had to face her. "You lost the dream of a family and that's huge. You have to mourn that and you and Reed need to do that together. You're so lost right now you don't know whether you're coming or going. The Kaylee I used to know wouldn't need to be told this and that's how I know that the desolation and grief that you're feeling is going to pass. I don't know how long it will take but I know that you're still in there. You. And you matter. You can't have a baby but we all love you. Our affection doesn't hinge on you birthing a child. It never has. That was an idea that you built up in your head. It's not true and it never was."

All the words that Kaylee had wanted to hear. She desperately wanted to believe them. More than anything, she wanted to believe that somewhere deep inside the woman she'd been was still in there. She'd be older, wiser, and a little more sad, but she'd be there. Somewhere along the line Kaylee had lost track of her.

"Sometimes I torture myself with might-have-beens," Kaylee admitted. She'd never admitted this to anyone. "Maybe I shouldn't have drank that coffee or maybe I should have exercised more. Or less. Maybe I shouldn't have had a glass of wine with dinner. Or I should have eaten more broccoli. I should have lost weight or not eaten that chocolate cake."

"You were looking for a reason," Ava replied, her voice growing thick with emotion and tears sparkling in her eyes again. "But sometimes there isn't a reason. I'm so sorry that life has dealt you these cards. I think you and Reed would have made amazing parents. You have such a wonderful loving instinct around Brianna and Colt. Life is so unfair and I'm so very angry that you aren't going to get to experience this."

Kaylee's eyes welled with tears. She was amazed she had any left to give. "I'm angry, too."

"Do you think Reed is angry at you? Or at life? I know that before him you hadn't had a lot of luck with the men in your life, first your father and then David. But Reed is different. He's not going to leave you when life isn't perfect. Is that what you think he's going to do? Bail when the road gets rocky?"

"Yes, but now you make me rethink that. I understand that he might need to…process all of this."

"Good, then this entire discussion has made some progress. Reed is angry at life, not at you. He doesn't hate you, although I can see that you've been hating on yourself. You've made this all your fault. Has it occurred to you that Reed might be the one that can't have children? After all, it was unexplained."

"They checked him out. They didn't find anything."

"They didn't find anything with you, either." Ava gave Kaylee a watery smile. "Am I boggling your mind with all of this logic? You've twisted yourself up in knots about this. Have you talked to anyone? You know, a professional."

"I went to a support group once." Kaylee shuddered remembering the room full of crying women. "It was horrible. I can't talk about my problems to strangers."

"No, you're not the type," Ava agreed. "Maybe you need to see a psychologist. One on one. Or with Reed. As I said, you both need to get on the same page. He's been hurting, too."

"And I haven't exactly been seeing anything outside of myself."

"I'm not an expert in this but I think your reaction is natural. It's just gone on too long without professional intervention."

"And I've spiraled down," Kaylee finished for her friend.

"I'm a fucking mess is what I am."

Ava swiped at her cheeks with a fresh tissue. "We both are at the moment. My heart hurts for you and Reed. I wish I had known earlier."

"I wish I'd told you earlier instead of letting this fester and bring me to this point."

Kaylee was tired of being tired. Of feeling like she was a failure and that her life didn't matter.

"I have to find a way to live my life without having a child," she said. "And I never thought I'd say that. I always thought my career would be enough and then I met Reed. We had so many dreams and plans."

"You'll get new plans and dreams."

"I want something to be hopeful about. Something to look forward to. And I feel so selfish throwing all my issues on you when you have your own problems. You're just trying to stay alive."

"And here you are helping out," Ava said with a laugh. "Risking your life, too. Maybe you're more alive than you think you are. Or maybe you wanted to be near Reed. That's a hopeful sign."

Kaylee did want to be near her husband. More than ever. She wanted to console him and soothe his pain. Ava had made a good argument. They should be doing this together, but Kaylee had been pushing him away over and over again. It was a miracle that her husband hadn't given up altogether and walked away.

Could they have a second chance? She had to try. The worst that could happen? Reed would push her away, confirming all that she'd thought for months. But maybe he still loved her and just maybe he could contemplate a life where it was just the two of them. It wouldn't be what they'd planned but Ava was right. They could make new ones.

Kaylee simply had to take that first scary step...

CHAPTER SIX

They hadn't made any progress finding Wade after discovering Marilyn's body. Reed had sat with Logan for hours poring over maps, conjecturing as to where Bryson might go next. They'd narrowed it down to two directions and each team was on the killer's tail, but Logan was frustrated with himself that he couldn't be more help. There were many lives on the line and Logan had taken all of them onto his shoulders, which was crazy. Wade Bryson was responsible for the mess. Logan was simply trying to clean it up before the body count was too high.

Reed's steps slowed as he approached his bedroom door. He was dog tired and wanted to catch a nap before dinner, but he'd seen Kaylee earlier in the day and her eyes had been swollen and red. More crying. He ought to be more sensitive to her moods, but he had a feeling she'd poured her heart out to Ava and told her friend what a lousy husband he was. He hadn't encouraged Kaylee to talk to her friend about what they'd been going through, although he couldn't think of the reason why at the moment.

Personal. That was it. It was far too personal to be broadcasting out to their friends. This wasn't a complaint like he didn't buy her flowers on her birthday – which he didn't. This was far different. If she told Ava, eventually Ava was going to tell Logan. Then fuck it all, Logan might eventually say something to Reed.

The last thing Reed wanted to do was talk about this. He didn't even want to talk about it with Kaylee. He just wanted to pretend it hadn't happened and move on with their lives. Was that too much to ask?

With his hand on the doorknob, he hesitated for a long moment. Maybe a nap wasn't a good idea. Kaylee was on the other side of that door and he didn't want to argue with her. He was too fucking tired to deal with all their issues.

Exhaustion won, however, and he pushed the door open and found his wife lying on the bed with her laptop propped up on her legs, typing away. He hadn't seen this sight in a long time. She looked up, her hands still poised over the keys.

"Hi."

"Hi."

He was an eloquent son of a bitch. He couldn't even talk to his own wife.

"I was just working a little bit."

"I was hoping to get a quick nap before dinner, but I can come back."

There was probably a chair he could sack out on downstairs.

She shook her head, her silky auburn hair catching the rays of the sun that were streaming in the window. "No, you can lie down. I can just read."

She set her laptop off to the side and picked up her e-reader. Left with no choice, Reed closed the door behind him and then eased himself onto the bed as close to the edge as he could get without falling off. Kaylee had made it clear to him months ago that she didn't want him touching her anymore.

Turning onto his side, he tried to get into a comfortable position, but the pillow was too hard and the bed not quite right. Honestly, he didn't sleep all that well when he wasn't cuddling his wife, even after all these months.

"Reed?"

Kaylee's voice was soft, lacking the hard edge he heard so much these days.

"Hmmm?"

"I'm sorry."

Before he'd left their home, Kaylee said she was sorry to him about a dozen fucking times a day. Usually he couldn't understand what she was sorry for and today probably wasn't going to be any different. But damn, he was going to ask anyway.

"About what, honey?"

For a moment he didn't think she was going to answer but then she did, her voice quiet in the silence.

"For being cruel to you. For being self-involved and full of self-pity. For letting myself spiral down to the point where I don't know what to do anymore. I'm so full of pain every single day and I guess somewhere along the line I forgot that you were, too. I'm so sorry about that. You deserved better from me and you didn't get it. If I could take it all back I would, but of course I can't. I can only tell you that I'm sorry and that I see your pain and hurt, too. I wish I could take it away."

This. This he'd never heard. Logan might have taken the brunt of the investigation onto his shoulders, but this little slip of a woman had taken the weight of the world onto hers. He rolled over so he could look into her eyes. They were bright with unshed tears, but she didn't seem as overwrought as she had in the past. If anything, she looked far more calm than she had in months.

"Honey, what I feel isn't your fault."

"I know, but—"

He shook his head. "But nothing. It's not your fault. This isn't anything you can snap your fingers and take away. If you could, I would have done the same for you. I know you're in a world of hurt, too."

She nodded, her head hanging low. "And I pushed you away when you wanted to comfort me. I shouldn't have done that."

No, she shouldn't have but he hadn't exactly been a knight in shining armor. He was supposed to save his wife from the big bad world but instead she'd been flung into it headfirst.

"I shouldn't have let you."

Lifting her head, she gave him the first smile he could remember seeing in a long time. "I don't think I gave you much of a choice."

"You're a stubborn one, that's true. But I didn't have to let you. I should have hung in there."

Because Kaylee had trouble trusting that he *would* be there. He should have remembered that.

Her fingers pleated the hem of her pink cotton tank top. "I pushed you away because I thought you hated me."

What in the ever-loving fuck?

"I could never—"

"No, Reed. Listen to me. You didn't see yourself that day at the doctor's office. You looked…different. Angry. Then you locked yourself away for days. I tried to get to you, but you were off somewhere. I thought you hated me. Do you? Maybe just a little?"

This was his doing. His huge mistake. He'd stuck a knife in his own wife's heart and then walked away, wondering why she was bleeding and crying. If he lived to be a hundred and fifty years old he could never make this up to her. She'd needed him and he hadn't been there. The one time Kaylee had needed her husband more than anything and he'd been MIA.

Because it had been tough. And difficult. And emotional. He'd done exactly what she'd feared he would do.

"Not in this lifetime. I love you more than I can ever express. You're more than just my wife, honey. You're my partner. You waited for me when you didn't have to. Understood me when any other woman would have given up. But you're right— I was angry. Angry at the world and the injustice I was feeling. But I was never angry at you. I was angry for us. For you. I know that you wanted a baby."

"You did, too."

He had. Still did, if he were being honest. Just because that wasn't in the cards didn't mean the wanting disappeared.

"I did, but most of all I just want you. I want us back where we were before. I want us to be happy again."

"I think I've forgotten how."

"Let me help you." He moved closer to Kaylee, slowly and cautiously, not wanting to spook her. They'd made progress in the last few minutes and he didn't want to fuck that up. "Honey, let me hold you. I think we both need that."

She didn't move closer to him, but she didn't jump off of the bed, either. She simply laid still as he slid his arm under her back and pressed his front to her side. She was stiff but that was a small issue. He was holding his wife for the first time in months. That was a victory he would savor.

Eventually she set her e-reader onto the nightstand and then with the sweetest of sighs her muscles went limp and she turned into him, her nose pressed against his chest. His arms instinctively tightened around her and he took a deep breath, filling his lungs with her unique scent of vanilla and rain. He remembered smelling it for the first time that day in her living room when she'd told him she didn't need his help. He'd been a goner for her practically from that moment.

With the soft warm bundle of woman in his arms, Reed was content. With a smile curving his lips, he closed his eyes and fell asleep.

There was light at the end of the tunnel. And it wasn't a train.

CHAPTER SEVEN

Logan stared at the map displayed on the huge screen on the wall. He'd been looking at it for a long time. Too long, really. His vision had gone blurry and his neck hurt.

No fucking progress.

He could stare at the map all day long, but the answer wasn't going to jump out and smack him over the head. He wanted to beat the shit out of Wade and that anger had taken up residence in his aching shoulders.

"You need to take a break."

His amazing wife was surely right but somehow he couldn't seem to stop. He wanted all of this to come to an end so he could take his family home. Or maybe to Disney. They deserved something good after dealing with his crappy past.

Ava held out a mug of steaming coffee. "This might help."

He accepted it, looking over the rim to check the contents. "I don't suppose there's any whiskey in here?"

"No, but I can get some if you want. Spoiler alert. I don't think booze is going to help. Caffeine might, though. It's always been my go-to answer when I'm stuck on a story."

"This isn't writer's block."

"Isn't it?" She perched on the edge of the desk and turned her gaze to the map. "You're trying to see the next steps that your antagonist is going to take. Isn't that exactly what you're doing here? Trying to keep up?"

"I'd love to be one or two steps ahead," Logan snorted. "But you do make an interesting comparison, wife. If Wade were the villain in one of your mysteries, what do you think he'd do next?"

"He'd never be a villain in one of my mysteries. Fiction has to make sense and reality doesn't always do that. My killers commit murder because of the usual reasons. Money, revenge, love. There are other reasons but those are the big ones. Wade, on the other hand, is playing on a whole different field. His reasons for killing aren't logical except to him." She tapped her chin and smiled. "Having said that, if I were ever so foolish as to write a character like Wade I'd think his next move would be to send you a message. He'd want to show off, make you afraid. He wants to be better than you, so he'd want you to know how great and wonderful he is."

"That makes sense. Do you think Marilyn's death was a message?"

Ava shook her head. "No, she has no real connection to you and the body dump site didn't either. I'd think he'd go someplace that you both remembered. That had meaning to you."

"That would be back to Corville and I can't see him heading there. He'd be spotted too quickly. The fact is I can't see how he's traveling around now. His face is plastered on the news several times a day."

"He may have altered his appearance," Ava warned. "Dyed his hair. Maybe a fake tattoo. He could even pad his clothing to make him appear heavier."

"I never thought that Wade could be this smart," Logan

marveled. "I thought he was a soft, rich businessman. Now he's a cunning killer on the run from the law and a master manipulator of people that should fucking know better. I never saw it coming."

"I'm guessing that he saw his father manipulate his mother for years before he pushed her off of that balcony. In business he probably needed to find the weakness in people and exploit it. Then he went to prison and received an education on how to do all of that on steroids. I didn't see it coming either but if I've learned anything from this it's that you never really know your friends. You can spend years with someone, but we don't know anything about what's going on in their private lives. Not unless they show it to us."

That was a strange statement for Ava to say. "Where did that come from? You don't usually talk this way."

"Let's just say that I was surprised today."

There was only one person here in this house that could do that.

"Is Kaylee okay?"

There was a long pause before Ava answered. "I don't know, but I think she will be. I'm worried about her. And Reed, to be honest."

"Reed? He seems fine."

"He does and that's why I'm worried."

Logan had long ago learned not to question his wife when she was like this. He trusted his gut as a lawman and he trusted Ava's gut about their family and friends.

"Is there some way we can help them?"

His wife's smile faded, her lips turned down at the corners. "No, and that's the shitty part. All we can do is be there for them. Listen and encourage. It would be great if we could wave a wand and make it all better, but we don't have that power."

"Maybe there's something. Let me know. They're our friends." He didn't want to make the offer but he did anyway. "I could talk to him, if you want me to."

"You hate talking about your feelings. I'm sure Reed does, too. No, we need to stay out of this. They need to work through this together."

"Whatever you say, boss."

That made the smile reappear. "Damn right. Now tell me what you're looking at here. Is that red dot the last sighting of Wade?"

There had been many Wade sightings. Too many to count. He couldn't be in all of those places at the same time. "That's where the vehicle and Marilyn's body was found. I'm trying to figure out where he might go next."

"Here?"

"You'd think that's where he'd head but the tip line has sightings going in the opposite direction. I'm thinking you may be right. He's going to show off a little bit before he comes here for me. The question is what is he going to do next?"

"Well, let's think about this. Wade never really matured after he saw his mother being murdered by his father. He sort of got stuck back there. Did anything happen that year that you can remember? Or that Wade would definitely remember? Did he win a science fair medal or get cut from the soccer team? How about a girl he had a crush on or a favorite place to go fishing?"

It was so long ago. How was Logan supposed to know what was important to a little shit like Wade? He'd always been an arrogant prick even when they were kids. He'd liked showing off how rich–

Wait a second. Wade liked showing off how rich his daddy was... Logan, on the other hand, never had any money. They'd grown up as brothers but that had been a line between the two of them that Logan couldn't cross. There were some things that Wade was able to do that Logan couldn't.

Like go to summer camp.

"You're thinking about something," Ava said, excitement rising in her tone. "I can tell by the look on your face. What is it?"

"Right after Wade's mom died, his dad sent all three brothers to summer camp. At the time I thought it was stupid as shit. We lived in Montana, for fuck's sake, in the middle of nowhere. Every day was summer camp. But his dad was adamant, so they went to this fancy camp near Yellowstone. It was for rich kids. I know that because Wade wanted me to be able to go so his dad offered to send me. He talked to my mom about it but she wouldn't do it." Ava was giving him a strange look. "I know what you're thinking. He was my dad too, but I just don't think of him that way. He was Wade's dad and my mother's killer. That son of a bitch is no relation to me."

She nodded and then stood, walking over to the wide screen on the wall. "So where is this camp? Do you think Wade would go there?"

Logan also stood and pointed to the spot on the map. "It's definitely a possibility. Griffin and Jason are headed that direction. I think they need to go there as quickly as possible."

Ava's brows shot up and the blood drained from her face. "Oh my God, are there kids there still? Would Wade hurt children?"

Wade had a strange sort of honor code. A weird one, but he followed it just the same.

"I don't think so, but where there are kids there are going to be adults." Logan pulled his phone from his shirt pocket. "I'm going to warn Griffin and Tanner, and I have you to thank."

"It was the least I could do."

"You're brilliant."

"I know."

"And beautiful."

"Of course."

"And modest."

That made Ava laugh as she turned toward the door. "I'm that, too. I'll leave you to make your calls. Do you want me to send Jared and Reed in?"

"Yes, please."

A lead. Finally. It wasn't for sure, but it was more than they'd had fifteen minutes ago. It was handy to be married to a murder mystery author. Ava just might have saved some lives this afternoon.

CHAPTER EIGHT

Amy and Mike carried in two large cardboard boxes and placed them on the floor next to the desk where Logan, Jared, and Reed were meeting after talking to Griffin and Jason. The two men were on the road and headed directly to the summer camp as fast as they could get there.

"Mail," Mike announced. "Specifically mail to Bryson while he was in prison."

"We've already seen it," Logan said. "Marilyn sent it to us. There's nothing there."

Amy reached into one of the boxes and pulled out a handful of letters. "No, you saw what Marilyn wanted you to see. There's a hell of a lot more. There are several more boxes that we need to bring in. The bastard was popular with the crazies. They'd send him letters, pies, knitted scarves, and then some weird shit like photos of them torturing their cat. Those never made it to him, but the prison kept them."

"Son of a bitch," Reed muttered under his breath. "The world is a sick place."

Maybe it was just as well that he and Kaylee weren't going to have any children. Why bring them into a society with all of this depravity?

"It is," Mike confirmed. "Should we bring in the rest of the boxes?"

"Absolutely," Logan said. "We need to look through those as quickly as possible. All hands on deck. We'll get Ava and Kaylee to assist."

"Are you sure?" Amy asked, hesitating in the doorway. Mike, on the other hand, had immediately jogged outside to start unloading the boxes. "It's just...Kaylee doesn't really have any experience doing this. I understand wanting to have Ava help but maybe it's not a good idea. I could call and have a couple of marshals here in the morning."

Reed glanced at Logan and Jared, gauging their reaction. As far as he was concerned, Kaylee knew enough about what was going on to be able to look through mail for someone who might have helped Bryson. But this wasn't his rodeo... It was Logan's call.

Jared was the first to speak. "Tomorrow morning will be too late. We need to look through that mail now and stay up until it's done."

Logan nodded in agreement. "Exactly, plus Ava and Kaylee aren't exactly clueless when it comes to this stuff. They'll do fine."

"Your call."

Turning on her heel, Amy strode out of the room without another word. Jared's brows rose and then he chuckled.

"Looks like we pissed her off."

Logan shrugged, putting his attention back on the map on the wall. "I can't worry about her delicate feelings. She's not in charge here and if that's an issue for her she's welcome to call her superiors and get another assignment."

"I'll go help," Reed offered. "The sooner we get started the better."

Jared quickly stood, pushing his chair back. "You stay here. I'll go help."

Confused, Reed could only nod as Jared followed after Amy.

"Is he worried about my back or something? I can carry a few boxes."

Reed had thrown his back out about a year ago, but he was fine now as long as he didn't do anything stupid. Like play football on Thanksgiving Day with a bunch of guys who were much younger than he was. Which was exactly how he'd hurt himself in the first place. To be fair, Kaylee had warned him it wasn't a good idea, but his ego hadn't wanted to admit that he was over forty and slowing down a bit. As usual, she'd been right.

Logan cleared his throat noisily and grimaced. "No, but he is worried that Amy is spending a little too much time with you. Whenever you two are in the same room she can't seem to tear her eyes from you."

"I'm not interested in her."

"We're not saying that you are. We're saying that she's interested in you. I don't think it's something we should be encouraging, unless you have other ideas."

Was Logan truly asking what Reed thought he was?

"I am not encouraging that woman. I love my wife."

"I know you do but we've noticed that Amy seems to like you. A lot."

Blowing out a breath, Reed slumped against the desk, draping a leg over the corner. "She's been...friendly."

"Is that all?"

"Yes. She offered me a sympathetic ear." Reed rolled his eyes. "Jesus, I'm not interested and I'm not even sure she's attracted to me. She's a nice woman. We may all be blowing this out of proportion."

"That's true. She does seem to gravitate toward you, though. I think she's a good agent but I also think she might have a...crush."

"I guess people can tell about Kaylee and me."

"To be fair, I didn't until Ava pointed it out," Logan explained. "My mind has been elsewhere these past few days. I'm sorry you two are going through a rough patch. I'm sure it will all work out."

"It will," Reed said with far more confidence than he possessed. Despite Kaylee allowing him to hold her for the first time in months, it didn't mean that their relationship was all patched up. They still had problems. "We're already doing better. Every marriage has its issues. We'll get through it."

"Just know that we're here for you. If you need it. But it sounds like it's all going to be okay."

"It is. For sure." The sound of footsteps in the hall had them both looking toward the door. "I appreciate the concern, though. You guys are good friends."

Reed wasn't sure how to fix his marriage but spending time with another woman absolutely wasn't going to help. He'd avoid Amy for the rest of his time here. He didn't need another problem on top of the ones he already had.

Reed had attracted the attention of many women over the years and for the most part Kaylee hadn't minded. She'd known that her husband wasn't interested and would be in her bed each night, so why worry?

Do I need to worry now?

"I can't believe you haven't smacked the crap out of her yet. I admire your restraint."

While they were all combing through Wade's prison mail, Kaylee had sought peace and quiet folding towels in the laundry room. She should have known Ava would find her.

"I don't know what you're talking about."

Ava shut the laundry room door behind her and leaned a hip against the washer. "You had a deep-seated need to fold laundry at midnight?"

"It needed to be done."

"It could be done in the morning. Those towels weren't going to jump out of the dryer and dance around. They'd be there whenever we got to them."

The image of the sunny yellow towels doing a dance down the hall had Kaylee giggling. "If they could dance they could fold themselves."

Ava sighed and rubbed at the back of her neck. "Wouldn't it be great if towels and clothes were self-folding? That's the worst part of doing laundry. If Logan had his way he'd never hang anything up. He'd just wear the clean clothes I bring upstairs in the laundry basket. When it's empty it must be time to do the wash again."

"Reed's more persnickety. He likes his clothes a certain way."

They'd come to the end of the laundry discussion because Ava threw a glance over her shoulder toward the door. "Amy likes him."

"I'm not worried about her."

Much.

Wrinkling her nose in distaste, Ava make a gagging noise. "She's trying to stay professional but it shows. And don't think that Logan and Jared haven't noticed. They have, and my husband mentioned that tomorrow he'd make a few calls and get Amy reassigned. Her crush on your husband isn't good for this mission."

"She thinks I'm only good for folding laundry."

Kaylee's tone was far more bitter than she'd intended but she'd had quite enough of Amy batting her eyelashes at Reed.

Especially when I'm standing right there.

"And we know better," Ava declared. "Don't worry about her. Reed isn't interested."

"She's a good marshal and she actually seems…nice."

"Well…yes. She's nice but she's also making a fool of herself." Ava took a step forward and lowered her voice. "Just ignore her because that's what your husband is doing."

"Is he? Are you sure?"

That green-eyed monster had Kaylee firmly within its grips and she hated what she'd become. One of those jealous women who didn't trust their husbands. She'd never thought she'd get here to this awful place.

But here she was.

"Reed would never cheat on you."

He was the most honorable man Kaylee had ever known. But Amy…

"She doesn't look like a quitter."

"She looks like a fool."

Ava's tone had Kaylee laughing. "I sure as hell won't argue with you about that."

Taking the towel from her hands, Ava nudged Kaylee toward the door. "Now go out there and don't give a shit what that woman says or thinks. She's not important. You and Reed are."

Kaylee didn't want to give up the progress she and her husband had made this afternoon. For a while today she'd felt…happy and content. A state she hadn't experienced in too long. Now she was greedy for more.

She'd found a little bit of hope here in this safe house.

CHAPTER NINE

Reed was tired and not in the best of moods. He wanted to be curled up in bed with his wife, not sifting through letters sent to Bryson from some of the wackiest people in the world. People who had real mental health issues and needed immediate professional intervention and care. It wasn't just the women fantasizing about reforming Bryson, it was the crazy monsters who fantasized about killing others in his name. Reed didn't even want to think about how many of these nut cases who had stopped thinking about it and made it a grisly reality.

After their tender afternoon together, Reed wanted more of Kaylee. Impatient as hell with the entire situation, he hadn't been the nicest to Amy this evening. To be fair, she hadn't made it easy. She didn't appear to be getting the message and he was going to have to be more direct with the female marshal.

Very direct. And if she still didn't get it, he'd draw her a fucking picture. Thank goodness, she'd finally gone outside to speak with Mike who was on guard duty.

Stretching his stiff back, he tossed the last letter on his stack into a box. There were plenty more still to go through, but they were making progress. "I'm going to make a fresh pot of coffee.

I could use the caffeine."

"I'll be in to get a cup in ten minutes," Jared replied with a yawn. "Make it industrial strength."

"Like tar," Logan agreed. "I'm fading fast. Why can't I be like the twins? A little sugar and they're good to go for hours."

"Because you're not six anymore," Ava teased him, kissing his cheek as she and Kaylee re-settled into chairs around the desk. They'd been off folding laundry or something like that for awhile, but Reed was glad to see his wife back. She was smiling too, and it was doing funny things to his heart. He loved this woman so damn much. It had to be obvious to the world.

"In other words, I'm getting old," Logan laughed. "It happens to everyone I guess but I thought my loving wife would be the last one to remind me."

"I'm getting old, too," Ava laughed. "You're not alone. Besides, I don't want to think about the alternative."

"Damn right," Jared said. "Getting old is a good thing. That's a birthday gift you don't want to give back."

Standing, Reed stretched his arms over his head, working out the kinks in his neck and back. "One pot of coffee coming up."

Bravely, he dropped a kiss on the top of Kaylee's head as he headed to the kitchen. As always, she smelled amazing and he was tempted to sweep her up in his arms and carry her to their bedroom.

Patience. I need more patience.

They'd made huge progress today but that didn't mean that she was ready to do more. He needed to move slowly, or he'd scare her off and they'd be back where they'd started.

"A cup of coffee sounds good."

Shit. He couldn't seem to shake this woman.

He flipped the switch on the coffeemaker and turned around to find Amy. She certainly was persistent.

"It will be ready in about ten minutes."

"I can wait."

She could but she didn't need to. Reed wasn't attracted to Amy, but he didn't want anyone else to think that he might be. Already they were talking about her behavior. She didn't know it, but Jared was going to call Evan tomorrow and have her reassigned.

"You seem tense."

Because you won't get the message.

"I think we're all tense. We want Bryson back behind bars so we can all go back to our regular lives."

The problem with Amy was that she wasn't a bitch or anything. If she had been, this would be easy. She truly seemed sympathetic.

"You're not happy."

Even when his relationship with Kaylee had been at its worst he'd been happy and grateful to have her for a wife and be sharing his life with her. That meant he needed to be blunt and kind of mean to Amy. Right now. He couldn't let her harbor any thoughts that this could ever be more.

"That's where you're wrong. I'm very happy. Maybe you simply don't recognize it when you see it." He walked up to her, invading her personal space. As a cop he'd learned about intimidating with his size early on. "I'm only going to say this once so listen up. I'm not interested. I will never be interested."

Whatever Amy might have said in response would forever be a mystery. Jared, Logan, Ava, and Kaylee stomped into the kitchen, their voices announcing their arrival before he could see them. They were debating the merits of two television shows and whether one was better than the other. Kaylee and Ava were bound to win whatever the argument. They always did.

To his surprise, Kaylee walked straight to him and wrapped

an arm around his waist. A warmth spread through his chest and gut and a big smile bloomed on his face. The ice was finally beginning to thaw. Fuck, he should have encouraged her to talk with Ava a long time ago. Clearly a few days with her best friend had helped. Kaylee looked far more relaxed than she had in months despite the crappy situation they found themselves in.

"Hey, babe," he whispered, pressing a kiss to her temple. "We're almost done with the mail. You can go upstairs and get some sleep if you need to."

She shook her head, her silky auburn hair tickling his arm. "No, I'm good. I want to finish. But we are going to need that coffee. Ava and I thought we might get a tray of snacks going, too. Coffee on an empty stomach isn't a good idea."

"I can help," Amy offered. "Just tell me what to do."

Before Ava could answer, Jared stepped in. "Actually, we need you to give Mike a hand outside. He's due for a long break."

Reed had half-expected Amy to argue but she didn't hesitate, turning on her heel and heading back outside. He gave his friend a grateful look over Kaylee's head. They had each other's back.

Things were finally looking up. His wife didn't hate him and Logan had a lead on Bryson's whereabouts. If they could find the son of a bitch, Reed could take Kaylee back home. Their home.

He and Kaylee could start their life again.

CHAPTER TEN

It was almost four in the morning when they all crawled exhausted up the stairs to bed. As tired as Kaylee was – and there were zombies who had felt livelier – she also desperately wanted a quick shower. She was so hopped up on caffeine and sugar the heat of the water might calm her, helping her fall asleep more easily.

Reed had lingered in the hallway talking to Logan and Jared, so she took the opportunity to strip off and step under the hot, steamy water. While Reed had slept on the floor last night, she didn't think he was planning to do that now. She'd opened up the floodgates this afternoon by cuddling with him and she had no regrets.

But…

It was kind of scary. It had been months since the last time she'd shared a bed with Reed, not to mention made love with him. Eventually even the sex had become perfunctory, almost a chore. Their playful and passionate physical relationship had been reduced to a calendar-driven schedule. And romance? Forget about it.

Spontaneity had gone out the window. No sex three days

before she was fertile. A pillow under her hips that had cancelled out any more daring positions. Then afterward, she'd lie there for a long time, her legs in the air praying this time it would work.

It wasn't a great formula for feeling sexy and desired.

The bathroom had filled with steam and her muscles loosened under the strong hot spray. Sleep had never come easily to her but she might actually get a few hours before the twins wanted breakfast. Unlike the rest of them, Colt and Brianna had been put to bed on time. Ava had warned that while her kids might bemoan a regular schedule they also thrived on it, which was funny coming from her. Ava was quite orderly but when writing, schedules went right out of the window. She didn't have that luxury anymore.

Kaylee was rinsing the lather from her skin when the shower curtain was thrown back and Reed stood there, steam billowing around his too perfect body. A cool breeze wafted around her and she could feel her nipples pucker in response and goosebumps rise on her wet flesh.

I guess it would be stupid to try and cover any part of me with my hands. He is my husband and he's seen it all.

And touched it. Many times.

Instead she tried to brazen it out by scolding him, but she had the sneaking suspicion that her face was bright red. Hopefully, he'd think it was just from the heat. "Reed, you're letting in the cold air."

"Then I'll close the curtain."

Stepping into the bathtub, he pulled the curtain closed. He was close and intimate, and it was kind of scary and exciting at the same time. Everything was moving so fast. This morning she and Reed had barely been speaking to one another and now they were both naked in the shower. She loved her husband and had never stopped wanting him, but it felt awkward and strange. It had been so long.

Had they completely forgotten how to have sex spontaneously? She couldn't remember the last time they had, it had been so long ago. For the last several years they'd only done it when the calendar told them to. It was sad that they'd lost that spark of kink that had brought them together. They used to have so much fun with their sexuality. Reed had never made her feel like her wants and needs were in any way wrong or weird.

Hot and steamy, it felt like a world all to themselves. Kaylee wanted to shut the rest of the world out and, for a few minutes at least, forget all their troubles and strife. But mostly she wanted to *feel* something good again. She'd been in pain for too long.

She handed the bottle of body wash to Reed, trying to keep her gaze from resting on his body. Heaven forbid she be caught staring.

"I'm already done so you can take it."

"Did you get your back?"

She hadn't become double-jointed nor had her arms grown several inches during their separation.

His intention was clear, and she was captured by how his normally hazel eyes had turned a molten gold. She knew that look well.

"No."

"No?" Reed stepped back, his expression wary. He was giving her the time and space to turn him down.

She could totally say no and step out of the shower, get dressed, and go to bed. Reed would never press her for more than she was ready for.

I can say no. Walk away.

Or I can stay here and feel my husband's arms around me again. It's been so long.

Like all humans, Kaylee craved physical affection. She and Reed had had a tactile relationship, always cuddling and holding one another. She'd missed that and she craved it.

"No…I didn't get my back."

His features eased and he held up the body wash. "I can do it for you. If you like."

She would like but was she ready for this? Her hesitation must have cued him in to her predicament.

"Just your back."

Her heart in her throat, Kaylee slowly turned so she was facing the shower wall. "That would be fine."

With just a touch to her shoulder it was like a live wire had been run from her neck all the way down her spine. For such a big tough man he had such a gentle touch and those magic fingers massaged the lather into her skin, running up and down her back. Her knees went watery and she had to reach out and brace herself with a hand on the tile walls. Pressing her lips together to hold in her whimper of want, she closed her eyes and savored the sensation. Her pulse raced and her stomach tumbled but she didn't move away, determined to enjoy feeling good.

I do deserve happiness. I don't have to be miserable.

Kaylee was tired of punishing herself. She was a naturally happy and optimistic person when she wasn't tied into knots with hormones. Maybe she was finally coming up for air, but she wanted to find that person that she used to be.

I'll be different too, but I need to find that part of myself that loved life. I want to look forward to each day. I want to find the passion that I've lost.

For writing. For Reed. For everything.

His rough fingers brushed her hip as he placed the bottle on the little bathtub ledge. His hands wrapped around her long hair, scraping it back from her face so he could press his lips to her temple and then her cheek.

So tender. So sweet.

She had to take a deep breath and screw up her courage for the next words out of her mouth. It was like closing her eyes and walking into traffic.

"I could…do your back, too."

Her voice was high, squeaky but he was too polite to point it out. His lips were close to her hair and she felt the puff of air from his warm breath. "That would be nice."

It was going to be far more than nice. It was going to be her pleasure to run her hands all over Reed. She liked touching him as much as he liked touching her. Especially after making love, Kaylee used to run her fingers up and down his muscular torso delighting in the differences between them, exploring every dip and plane of his body. If she closed her eyes right now, she could still remember all of it. Every single inch.

Pouring some of the bath gel into her palm, she rubbed her hands together and then placed one on each of his shoulders. Her fingers glided over the muscles bunched at the base of his neck right where he carried all of his tension. There was so much more at stake than just their marriage. Reed had lives that depended on him.

Tentative at first and then growing bolder, Kaylee ran her hands down his spine to where it met his perfectly formed ass cheeks. It really wasn't fair how sexy he was or how he looked in a pair of well-fitting blue jeans.

I wonder if I'll still act like this when we're eighty.

Assuming we can get there. Together.

"That feels good, honey."

A wife always knew her husband's moods and tones. Reed was aroused and she could hear it in his voice. If he turned around she'd see his hard cock begging to be caressed and licked. Those golden eyes would have turned a tawny brown, almost like toffee.

"I'm glad," she whispered, although no one could hear them. It just seemed like the thing to do. "I can...do the rest."

Reed didn't answer right away, and she thought she might have misread his signals. It had been months after all, but then he turned around and he was exactly as she'd thought he would be. Hard, ready, with desire stamped on his features. He'd been holding himself in check. For her.

"Baby, I'm not sure I can take your soft hands on me much longer without doing something about it," he growled, frustration in his tone.

This was the crossroads. He was leaving the decision to her. What did she want to do?

I want to be with my husband.

Watching Amy flirt with Reed wasn't the main reason she wanted to be with him, but it had certainly shown her that she didn't want him with anyone else. She was jealous and possessive. Two qualities she wasn't fond of but there it was. She couldn't deny it.

Tentatively reaching out, she placed her hands on his chest. "I'm not saying no."

Even then, Reed didn't let himself off of the leash. He hesitated, confusion in his expression.

"But are you saying yes? I won't do anything that you don't want me to, honey. We've come too far since you arrived for me to mess it up because I'm impatient."

I'm impatient, too.

The words came out far stronger than she'd ever imagined they could. "I'm saying yes. This doesn't mean everything is fine. We have a lot of work to do, but it means that I want to do that work with you."

Clearly, she'd said the magic words. With another groan, he

swept her up into his arms, his mouth coming down onto hers. Their tongues played tag in that old as time game. Her fingers tightened on his shoulders and her legs turned to jelly as his lips slid down her neck to where her pulse beat wildly.

Dammit, that spot always made her eyes roll back into her head. Reed hadn't forgotten and was even nipping at it, making her squirm as her arousal built quickly. Now that she was in her husband's arms, she was hungry – no, make that voracious – for pleasure.

"Reed," she whimpered, her head falling back against the tile wall, giving her whole self over to the sensations crashing through her body. Pleasure bubbled through her veins like fine champagne as his lips closed around a tight nipple and his fingers found her wet and wanting. "I need you."

"I need you too, honey."

Those magic digits unerringly found her sweet spot and she would have fallen into a heap in the bathtub if his strong arms hadn't been holding her up. Placing an arm under her bottom, he lifted her off of her feet and pressed her back against the tile, his hard cock trapped between them. She tried to reach down and caress him, but he shook his head, his mouth leaving a damp trail to her ear.

"No, baby. If you touch me I'm going to go off like a rocket. I'm too close."

Kaylee was ready to fall over the edge as well. She'd denied her body pleasure for so long it was drinking it up like a parched man in the desert. Her nails dug into Reed's back and she shifted so that she could press even closer to his fingers that were doing devious things to her clit.

"Now, Reed. Fuck me now."

She sounded demanding but that's what she was. The temperature of the bathroom had gone up at least twenty degrees and she was on fire from the inside out. The water fell down on her fevered and sensitive flesh, amping up her arousal as his hands worked their usual magic. He knew every button to push, every spot that sent her into orbit.

His cock nudged at her entrance, pressing forward and then pausing when she had to catch her breath. Reed wasn't a small man and it had been months, but she was so wet it didn't take long for him to slid into the hilt. She moaned at the pleasure of being so full. It felt better than anything she could imagine, and it was the most intimate feeling with this man.

Because Reed liked to look into her eyes when he fucked her. Even now their gazes were locked as he pulled out and slammed back in, sending shivers up and down her spine. The coil of pleasure in her belly tightened with each thrust and she watched fascinated as his pupils dilated, almost obliterating the iris. He was close and so was she. With every stroke he was rubbing that spot inside of her while his thumb thrummed against her swollen clit. Trembling and shaking, she was teetering on the brink. A feather touch could send her over.

It was his words that did it. Burying his head in her neck, his teeth nipped at the skin right where he knew it would make her insane.

"I love you, honey. I love you."

Kaylee opened her mouth to declare her own love but the only thing that came out was Reed's name as her orgasm hit her hard, turning her upside down and sideways. Pleasure ripped through her body like a freight train and she gave herself over to it, knowing she was safe and cared for in Reed's arms. His own climax came on the heels of hers, muscles taut and his head thrown back in ecstasy. He was so incredibly beautiful at this moment, vulnerable, too. It was hard for a person to hide their emotions when they'd truly succumbed to the passion.

When they trusted their partner implicitly with their heart and soul.

He held her there for a long time, their breathing ragged and labored before eventually lowering her to the floor, making sure her shaky legs could hold her own weight. The water wasn't nearly as hot anymore, but it was warm enough that they could both clean up before stepping out of the shower. With such gentleness, Reed dried her off, tucking the towel around her and placing a soft kiss on her lips.

They hadn't solved all of their problems — they might even have made them worse — but Kaylee wasn't sorry. This was her first baby step back to happiness and love. She wanted to make her marriage work.

She was ready to fight for it.

CHAPTER ELEVEN

Kaylee slowly opened her eyes, the sunlight still weak through the gap in the curtains. It was early, and someone was knocking softly on their bedroom door. It had to be important to wake them up at dawn. They'd only had a few hours of sleep.

But she didn't want to wake up and start the day. She was tucked safely into Reed's warm body, his face buried in her hair and his arms wrapped around her like steel bands. In fact, she never wanted to move from this spot, breathing in his calming scent and feeling the rise and fall of his chest.

The world was insistent on intruding.

With a growl of frustration, her husband eased away to answer the door. "It has to be important, honey."

"I know."

Kaylee gathered the covers more closely around her now that she didn't have her furnace of a spouse keeping her warm. Whoever it was didn't come in, just whispered a brief message and left, their footsteps barely audible in the early morning quiet.

Reed shut the door, his expression tight. Whatever he'd been told hadn't been good news. Her empty stomach twisted with fear and foreboding. Something had happened.

"Honey, I need you to get up and get dressed. We need to pack. We're heading out as soon as we can. I'm going to go downstairs and get the details so just leave out a change of clothes for me, okay?"

A million questions ran through her head but she reined them in, knowing she'd eventually get all the answers she wanted and then some. Reed didn't have any details either; the visitor hadn't been there long enough to impart any. Whatever was going on though was bad enough that they were leaving and going elsewhere.

"Okay, it should only take me a few minutes. Then I'll help Ava pack up the kids' stuff."

He leaned down and pressed a sweet and slow kiss to her lips, reminding her of how he'd made love to her last night. She loved this man so much.

"I know Ava will appreciate the help. I'll come find you as soon as I can," he replied, dragging on a pair of jeans and a t-shirt. His feet were still bare and his short dark hair was askew. "It's all going to be alright. It's just a precaution."

This safe house was only a precaution. Did they need safety from the precaution?

When the door clicked shut behind him, Kaylee jumped out of bed and went straight into the bathroom to splash some water on her face, yawning the entire time. This day was going to suck. It had all the signs. No sleep. A mysterious visitor early in the morning. And now they were going to be packed into the car to travel…? Destination unknown.

As quickly as possible, Kaylee dressed and packed their belongings, leaving out a fresh change of clothes and a toothbrush for Reed. They hadn't brought much with them, so it didn't take long before she was knocking on Ava's door to help her.

"I think the twins have twice as many clothes as Logan and I put together," Ava sighed when Kaylee entered the room. Two large suitcases were lying open on the bed, along with stacks of clothing, and a scattering of books and toys. "When did that happen?"

"Because they get dirty easily and you didn't want to do laundry every single day," suggested Kaylee with a wry smile.

"True," Ava agreed. "How are you holding up?"

"Decent, but then all I know is that we're leaving. Do you have any other information?"

Ava glanced toward the door that separated the master bedroom from the adjoining room where the twins were still asleep. They wouldn't be for long, however. Now that the sun was up they'd be raring to go quite soon.

"Logan received a call not long ago from Griffin and Jason. They got to that summer camp. All the kids were fine but just outside the camp there was a fishing shack. They found two men there dead. Both shot."

"Bryson's message to Logan."

They'd been expecting it, but it was far more grisly than Kaylee had imagined it would be. She should have known better. Bryson was a cold-blooded killer.

"Wade left more than two dead bodies. He carved a message onto the chest of one of the dead men. It was the address of this house. He knows where we are."

Shuddering, Kaylee rubbed at the goosebumps that instantly rose on her arms. Bryson was also a sick bastard and his games weren't fun for anybody but him.

"So we have to leave."

"Yes," Ava nodded. "He could be on his way by now or he could be taking his time."

"Because he loves the chase," Kaylee finished for her friend.

"The game is everything," Ava agreed. "Cat and mouse and we're not the feline in this scenario."

"We should be."

"You're sounding a whole lot like my husband. He agrees wholeheartedly with you. He wants to go on the offensive. He hates playing defense."

"Then what's stopping him?"

Ava pointed to Kaylee. "Your husband. And Tanner, and Jared, and Seth, and–"

Kaylee held up her hands. "Okay, I've got it. How do you feel about this?"

Ava started tossing clothes into the suitcase. "It depends on when you ask me. One minute I think we should play it safe, and the next I'm so pissed off and tired I just want to go after the son of a bitch."

"I don't think Logan would let you go after Bryson."

Her fingers tight around an old t-shirt, Ava's knuckles were white with tension. "If I saw Wade Bryson, I'd kill him. No discussions, no stop or I'll shoot bullshit. He'll never stop until he's dead. We won't have a moment of peace if all they do is lock him up again. He's already shown that he can get out if he wants to."

"I heard Jared say that next time they'd send him to the Supermax in Colorado."

Kaylee had done some research about those kinds of prisons and they were truly for the worst of the worst. Wade wouldn't be holding court with a psychologist or other prisoners. He wouldn't have any contact with anyone but his attorney.

"I think Wade Bryson just might be the first prisoner to break out of that prison," Ava said between gritted teeth. "If anyone could it would be him."

"He's just a man," Kaylee reminded her friend. "He doesn't

have any special superpowers except that he has no conscience and no empathy."

"That makes killing easier for him."

Kaylee doubted Bryson cared about anything or anyone but himself.

"Do you know where we're going?"

Throwing the last piece of clothing into the suitcase, Ava began to stack up the books.

"I have no idea, but I can't wait to get there. How about I finish here and you go wake up the twins? I want them to have some breakfast before we get on the road. At least I hope we have time for that."

It sounded like the best plan they had. For now.

CHAPTER TWELVE

Logan wasn't one to wallow in self-doubt but today was the exception. Were they doing the right thing? There were pros and cons to the decision and they'd talked about them all, but he still wasn't confident that they'd made the right choice. What if he ended up getting his family or one of his friends hurt or killed? He wanted to be confident, but he had to admit that this situation had him sideways. He was so fucking sick and tired of it all. Wade would never give up as long as he breathed air and he'd always be a threat to Ava and the kids.

Logan stood firmly in between Wade and his family.

"We're almost ready to go," Reed said, joining Logan and Jared in the office. Amy and Mike were on guard duty around the perimeter. "The twins are finishing breakfast so maybe ten minutes?"

They'd been staring at the monitor on the wall again. The same map but this time they were looking for a safe destination.

"This sucks," Logan said flatly. "What a clusterfuck."

"It is," Jared agreed. "Are you worried about making a move in daylight? We could wait until tonight."

"I'm worried about goddamn everything," Logan replied, his

tone laced with bitterness. "He's had enough time to get here. That is, if he wanted to. But we don't know where he is. He's playing his games again. Shit, he could be photographing bears in Yellowstone like a fucking tourist while we scramble around trying to find somewhere safe. Or he could be sitting out there watching every move we make and when we leave he'll either ambush or follow us so he can keep fucking with me."

"If he's out there, we'll find him," Reed said confidently. "He can't hide forever."

"Can't he?" Logan asked, pointing to the map. "We don't know where he is and we're depending on a tip line and questioning people to find him. You would think with a reward on the line, someone would turn the bastard in but it's almost like the public is rooting for him to get away. And in the meantime, the body count climbs higher."

Jared stood and pointed to a spot on the map. The summer camp. "We know his last known whereabouts and that's more than we had a few hours ago. We also know that he stole a silver Honda minivan, which is a hell of a lot more than we knew before. We're getting tips in faster than we can process them. We'll get him. We're in a better position than ever."

Logan laughed but he really didn't think it was funny. "Jesus, you are such an optimist. We're like sitting ducks and you think we're winning the game."

"I think we are. He's one man. We have multiple teams searching for him."

Slapping his hand on the oak desk, Logan ground his teeth in frustration. "That's another thing that bugs the shit out of me. Wade has to have help. One man couldn't do this alone. Think about it. Transportation. Money. Food. Shelter. His face is plastered on every television and phone screen in three states."

"I agree," Reed replied, nodding his head. "But we've looked through all of Bryson's mail. It was sick as shit and the authorities have checked out the few people we flagged. Nothing."

"What about friends or family of Marilyn?" Jared asked. "Could he be getting help there? Or maybe someone that is or was employed at the prison. A guard or even a janitor or cook."

"We've checked them all out. There was nothing there. I only wish there was," Logan said, falling back into the soft leather chair. He was exhausted and he didn't have the answers that he needed to keep his family protected. He'd thought this would only last a few days, a little summer camping trip that the kids would love. But they were beginning to ask questions, wondering what was going on. They were smart. Hell, they were probably a hell of a lot smarter than he was and they knew something was going on. He had to get them back home and into their normal world and life as soon as possible. "I still hate this playing defense stuff. I think we need to get out ahead and take the offensive. Go after him."

Clearly Jared didn't like the idea. He jumped out of his chair and began to pace the small space.

"We already have several teams looking for him."

"I'm talking about baiting a trap. With me."

Jared was already shaking his head. "We are not going to do that. We said we'd keep you alive. That is dangerous and frankly we're getting too old for that shit. At least I am. Besides, Ava would cut off your balls and ours, too. Misty would help."

"Kaylee would as well," Reed agreed. "They're not thrilled about all this danger crap. But I might have an idea. It's a longshot..."

Logan was ready to hear any idea no matter how outlandish. "I'm listening."

"It might already have been done—"

"Maybe but let's hear it anyway. We could use a fresh idea or two."

Reed stood and walked over to the windows that overlooked the side yard. Mike could be seen from there keeping watch over the long driveway from a limb in a big oak tree. The marshal was as steady as they came and absolutely no nonsense.

"You say that we've checked out all of the employees of the prison. All of Marilyn's friends and family. We've read through all of the mail and the cops have checked out a few of the more menacing pen pals." Reed paused, scraping his hand down his face. "It's just I remember this one case I worked on when I was a rookie. The local body shop had a theft problem and they were convinced that it was an inside job. We agreed as there was never forced entry and the thieves always seemed to know where to find what they wanted. But it wasn't an inside job per se. It was a former employee from years before who had left town and returned. He knew enough about the business to easily steal and the owner hadn't ever changed anything, including the locks. The guy was able to use his old key that he'd never returned."

His brain working a mile a minute, Logan could see what Reed was trying to describe.

"You're saying that it might be someone who used to work at the prison?"

Reed nodded. "Or the county jail. Or even one of his transport details. We've checked out *current* employees and cops. What about the ones that were there when Bryson was first incarcerated?"

Jared looked like he was on board with the theory. "That's how he might have met them. We need access to former employee files. Everyone who might have had any sort of contact with Bryson."

Logan was excited about this new direction. It at least gave them a direction which he felt they were sorely lacking. "That could be a boatload of people, but I think you're onto something. If he made friends with someone inside besides Marilyn, they could be helping him now."

"I'll make the call," Jared said, dialing his phone. "Then we need to get out of here."

Wade knew where they were. Would he find them where they were going?

"We need to pick up camping gear along the way," Jared said, making a list as Reed and Logan packed the vehicles. They should have been on the road thirty minutes ago, but they'd argued about whether to head to a populated area or somewhere far more remote. Remote won. "And then we need to stop at a grocery store to pick up supplies."

Reed shoved the last suitcase into the trunk. "Can I ask a question? How come you're not lifting anything heavier than a pen and Logan and I are heaving luggage around?"

Grinning, Jared tapped his pen against the small tablet. "Because I'm the brains of the operation and you're the brawn."

Logan wiped his hands on a handkerchief from his pocket. "You are such an asshole. I don't know how Misty puts up with you."

"Frankly, I don't know either," Jared said. "Are we ready to go? It feels like we're never going to leave."

Logan nodded toward the house. "Let's get them loaded into the cars."

Jared loped off to round up the woman and children, but Logan placed a hand on Reed's arm staying his movement.

"Can we talk for a minute?"

"Of course."

"I know you think we should head for a population center

near law enforcement and hospitals."

Reed hadn't made any secret of that. During the discussion, he'd made his argument but lost.

"I get why you're against it. You have a point about innocent lives. I was thinking more about our lives, honestly."

"You made a good argument in there and the more I think about it the more I wonder if you're right."

Logan didn't change his mind without a damn good reason and Reed had a good idea why he'd done it.

"But not for everyone," Reed guessed. "You think that the women and kids should be in a more populated area."

"I do," Logan agreed. "When Griffin and Jason arrive, I want you and Jared to take our wives and the twins and put them on a plane to Florida where Evan can keep an eye on them. They'll be safe there."

"If that's what you think, then you should go, too."

His friend was already shaking his head. "I'm the target. And the bait. I have to stay here, but they don't have to. I need them out of the line of fire. I don't think you want Kaylee here any more than I want Ava and the kids."

Reed had been going back and forth about it. He loved having his wife there and they'd grown closer in the last few days, but as the danger had ratcheted up he'd thought more and more about sending her away. The only reason he hadn't done it was that he didn't think she'd go and leave her best friend.

"I don't but she's stubborn as hell. Ava is, too. She isn't going to want to leave you."

"I'm not planning on giving her a choice. Every day that Wade is on the loose becomes more dangerous for all of us. I can't put her and the kids in the line of fire. I want to keep them close. That's the selfish part of me. But deep down inside I know that they'd be better off away from me. Wade doesn't really want them. He wants me."

"So what do you want to do? Everyone thinks we're headed for the middle of nowhere."

"We are to a certain extent. We'll go to that cabin that Jared knows about and meet the others there. Then you'll take the women and children and get the hell out as soon as I can make the arrangements. I'll go after Wade and end this shit once and for all."

It sounded like a good plan to Reed but there was one problem... Two, actually.

"Our wives are never going to let you do it."

"I don't take my orders from Ava."

Despite the dire situation they were in, Reed couldn't stop the laughter that bubbled up. "Yes, you do. And I take orders from Kaylee. They're always right so we'd be fools not to listen. Once our women get wind of this plan they're going to barbecue your butt."

"I have an ace in the hole, my friend."

"Really? Do tell."

The twins were running toward them, Kaylee and Ava on their heels carrying two small backpacks – one pink and one blue.

"Them."

"Them?" Reed echoed. "I don't understand."

"Colt and Brianna. I'll tell Ava that the kids aren't safe near me. She'd take a bullet for those two, so she'll do whatever it takes to keep them safe. Even leave me."

"I hope you're right."

"I am. You'll see."

Considering that Ava and Kaylee always seemed to be one step ahead this ought to be quite interesting to watch play out.

Time to hit the road.

CHAPTER THIRTEEN

Kaylee could see the tension in her husband by the tightness of his jaw and the way his shoulders were set, so stiff and unyielding. They'd been on the road for about an hour and a half and he'd barely spoken a word except to Logan and Jared. Constantly on alert, he'd kept checking his rearview mirror as their vehicle was the "tail" of this small parade. Mike and Amy were in the front, Jared right behind, and Logan, Ava, and the twins next. From this distance, Kaylee could see the outline of her best friend in the passenger seat, her hands gesticulating in the air. Logan and Ava were having a lively discussion. Or maybe they were simply singing a song with their kids.

Giving up on the book she'd been trying to distract herself with, Kaylee gave all of her attention to her husband. She loved looking at him, studying his chiseled profile and enjoying the strength and integrity she saw there. Reed was a handsome devil and he only seemed to get better with age. There was silver at his temples and a few new lines around his eyes, but they only served to make him more interesting.

Why wasn't it the same with females? Men became more fascinating and women became...older.

Except that Kaylee didn't always feel just older. She'd walked through fire, and although the flames were still lapping at her heels she just might make it to the other side, scarred but alive. Ava had reminded her that she was strong and could handle this.

I'm going to be okay. Somehow. Eventually.

Either with Reed or without him. Kaylee would prefer it to be with her husband, but she was so tired of apologizing for something she couldn't control or fix. This was who she was and if he didn't want her this way she'd have to find a way to deal with it. They were both hurting and instead of moving toward each other, they'd both curled into a ball and turned away. Finding each other in the dark wasn't going to be easy but she was willing to reach out and so was he. They had a chance and for that she was grateful.

"Are we being followed?" she asked as he glanced in the rearview mirror again.

His head jerked in her direction, his brows pulled together in a frown. "No. Hell no. Why do you ask?"

"Because you keep looking in the mirror. I assume you're concerned about being followed."

Sighing, his shoulders relaxed for the first time that morning. "Yes and no. There was a concern that Wade was watching the house and might follow us when we leave but we haven't seen any sign of that. I think we got away clean."

"Got away clean," she repeated, amusement in her tone. "Such a charming expression. Like we just knocked over a bank and are on the run from the heat."

Reed smiled, showing off his dimples. "Baby, I am the heat."

Remembering last night, she could only agree. "Yes, you are."

His hazel eyes had darkened to almost black. He too was thinking about last night.

"When we get home I am going to make you scream my name over and over. The neighbors will know I'm back."

They hadn't discussed Reed that but she wasn't against it. They couldn't work this out separately and they were both miserable apart.

"Our closest neighbor is over three miles away, Reed."

Chuckling, he shot her an evil grin. "You're going to be screaming pretty loud."

Something to look forward to, but...

"We still have a lot to work out. It's not all fixed because we had sex last night."

"I know. But we're not solving anything with me living in the apartment above the station. We need to be together. Or rather, I need to be with you. I hope you feel the same."

"I do."

"But?"

Kaylee shook her head. "No buts. I just know that we have a lot of work ahead of us. There are still things we need to talk about. I'm so tired of crying. Everyone talks about how cleansing it is and I know it can be, but lately I don't feel any better after a good cry. I just feel..."

"Sad?" Reed finished for her. "Exhausted? More confused than ever?"

"That about covers it. How did you know?"

"You're not the only one who has cried."

Reed had cried? She'd certainly seen her husband shed a tear or two but an actual crying jag?

"I'm sorry I made you cry."

"I'm sorry too, although it wasn't so much what we did to each other, was it? Life isn't going to let us have the fairy tale and that hurts like a bitch, but we have so much else to be thankful for. That's what I want us to concentrate on. What we have, not what we don't."

It sounded so easy but doing it was far more difficult.

"I am grateful for what we have. I know how lucky we are. And yet—"

Kaylee broke off, loath to put her thoughts into actual words.

"You're still upset that we can't have it all."

"Yes," she admitted, her voice shaky with emotion. Her throat had tightened up and she had to swallow hard to be able to speak. "I know that's selfish. We have so much and so many have so little that it feels petty to be like this. To want more."

"It's not petty. It's human."

"It still feels wrong."

"You're so hard on yourself. Far harder than anyone else could ever be. Cut yourself some slack. You're only human. We both are."

To lighten the atmosphere, Kaylee tried to crack a joke. "This is why I don't read my reviews."

"I've read them. Readers love you."

"I bet they don't all love me."

Shrugging, he glanced in the rearview again but this time much less tense. "Probably, but they don't matter. Not everyone is going to love you, honey. Life doesn't work like that."

"If I remember correctly, that's how you and I met. Nasty letters from a so-called fan. I know that everyone isn't going to love me, but it would sure be nice."

Kaylee still read all of her emails – good and bad. Most of them were good but a few were blisteringly awful.

"You wouldn't want that. If everyone loves you, you're kissing somebody's ass. And you're no ass-kisser."

Neither was he.

"Interesting theory you have there. I never thought about it that way, but you have a point."

"I'm a wise man."

He'd said it with such a straight face Kaylee had to laugh. "That you are. Now can the wise man shed some light on a question that's been bugging me?"

"Absolutely."

Kaylee pointed to the vehicle in front of them. "What's going on there? Ava looks animated."

Reed gave a heavy sigh and then groaned. "That poor dumb bastard. I bet Ava took one look at Logan and knew exactly what he's up to. He's screwed."

"What is he up to? Is he thinking about going after Wade again?"

"I wish it were that simple. He's got an idea that's not going to make Ava happy. You won't be, either."

"Then you better tell me all about it."

Kaylee stretched her cramped legs as she exited the car. They were stopping for gas and to grab a bite to eat. The twins were complaining that they were hungry and her own stomach was growling angrily. Even the fast food smelled amazingly delicious and she couldn't wait to sink her teeth into a cheeseburger and fries. Maybe a chocolate shake, too. She hadn't eaten much for breakfast, too anxious about their road trip.

The store they'd stopped at was one of those supermarts with gas, food, and a huge store with everything and anything they could ever want. Reed and Jared were going to follow the women around the grocery area while the others picked up camping gear. The cabin they were going to didn't have enough room for all of them to sleep inside. Luckily it wasn't January.

Not knowing how long they would be stuck there, Kaylee

and Ava piled the cart high with food – some healthy and some nothing but junk.

"Never go the grocery store hungry," Kaylee said, tossing two bags of chips into the cart. "Which is why we're going to spend a small fortune in this store. I'm starved."

"I am, too," Ava declared. "And I don't care how much crap we eat. If I'm going to be on the road like this, I'm going to have s'mores."

Reed and Jared flanked the women but stayed back a few steps, always watchful and on alert. For a short time, it was rather peaceful as the twins had whined until they got to go with daddy to look at tents. They'd thought that was the coolest thing ever.

"When we were driving behind you…well…it looked like you were upset about something." Kaylee kept her voice down so Reed and Jared wouldn't hear. "Reed said that Logan wants us away from him."

Ava rolled her eyes and sighed. "Yes, he does. I'm shocked he let the twins hang out with him in this store, but I guess he thinks that Wade isn't following us and that he wouldn't start a shootout in a superstore in Montana where everyone is packing heat."

"He's just worried about you and the kids."

For some reason Kaylee felt the need to defend Logan. Every time she looked at him, he appeared to be a man tortured by the current circumstances.

"I know and that's why I didn't cut off his balls. I simply let him know that I wasn't leaving him. The kids, on the other hand…"

Kaylee's ears perked up at her friend's words. Clearly Ava was having misgivings about keeping her children close. "You're thinking about sending Brianna and Colt somewhere else?"

Lips turned down, Ava rubbed at her temples. "I don't want to. My motherly instinct is to wrap them in cotton wool and keep them close to me, but like Logan says that might not be the smartest thing I could do. Being away from us would probably be safer. Evan has a group of former marshals in Florida that could watch over them. Heck, they could take them to Disney World. They'd love that."

"They'd miss their parents."

"When Mickey Mouse and all the princesses are there? Not hardly."

"You wouldn't go with them?"

It was hard for Kaylee to wrap her mind around the idea that Ava would let her children go. But if it was to keep them safe...

"Logan needs me. But they wouldn't go alone. They'd be with the person I trust most in the world."

It took a moment for Kaylee to realize that Ava meant her. She would trust her children to Kaylee even with a sadistic sociopath on the loose.

Overwhelmed with emotion, Kaylee's eyes welled with tears. "I would protect them with my life. You know that."

"That's why I could send them with you."

"But," Kaylee said, holding up her hand. "They would want their mom and dad. I'm a poor substitute."

"They love you," Ava insisted, looking right and left. The men were still hanging back and busy watching everyone else. "I know that this is a shitty time to discuss this but if anything happens to me and Logan–"

"Don't even say it. Don't even think it."

Ava stopped the cart near a tower of bananas. "No, I need to say this despite this being the worst location ever for a discussion like this. I should have done it long before now. If anything happens to Logan and me, we want you and Reed to raise our children. I should have asked you first but we kind of put that in our will. You have the choice, though. If you don't want to, then Jared and Misty are up to bat. My mom is getting too old to run after two kids and my sister hates my guts. You're like the sister I never had but always wanted. I know you'll do right by Colt and Brianna."

Tears streamed down Kaylee's cheeks and she quickly swept them away, not wanting to make a scene right here in the produce section. She bent her head hoping that Reed didn't see because he'd want to know what was happening.

"You certainly have lousy timing. We're shopping for oranges," she replied thickly, trying to make light of a serious situation. It was becoming a habit. "You know that we'd raise them as our own."

"I know you would, but I also don't want you to feel obligated to do it. That's why we've given you the option. I would understand if you didn't want the responsibility and expense. There would be insurance money, of course, and you could sell our houses—"

"Stop," Kaylee commanded loudly, drawing strange looks from passersby. Jared and Reed were eyeing them curiously as well and looked ready to intervene at any moment. "Seriously, stop talking about this. Nothing is going to happen. You and Logan are going to be fine and we're going to catch Wade and everything is going to be wonderful."

It sounded a little bit fantasy-like, but it was the outcome Kaylee was hoping and praying for.

She couldn't even fathom the alternatives. It all made her problems seem so small in comparison.

Reed sidled up to Kaylee and placed an arm around her shoulders. His gaze was searching, questioning, but this was far from the place to tell him the content of the conversation. "Is everything okay here?"

Both women nodded and smiled, Kaylee wiping away the last stray tear. Her heart felt too big for her ribs and her stomach tumbled in her abdomen. Ava was the closest thing she had to family and she would do anything for her.

"We're fine," Kaylee assured her husband. "We just had a moment. We're both hungry so we're going to hurry up here so we can eat."

Reed didn't believe a word out of her mouth. He'd always known her so well but to his credit he didn't call her out today. "Sounds good. We're hungry, too. What all is left?"

"Produce and meat," Ava pronounced. "Then we'll be finished."

Reed checked his phone. "The others are done too, so let's hurry. We need to get back on the road. We're too out in the open here."

Because they could never forget why they were all here together. Wade Bryson.

CHAPTER FOURTEEN

As far as fishing cabins went, it was nice. Two small bedrooms, a bathroom, and a large combination living room and kitchen. There were two old rocking chairs on the front porch and a cord of wood stacked up on the side of the house. As Jared had predicted it was empty, no smoke curling from the chimney. His friend that owned it was currently in Chicago at a forensics convention.

The cabin was nestled by a lake at the back and a long winding driveway from the main road. It was a compromise for the next twenty-four hours. Close enough to civilization that they weren't completely cut off but far enough away that no innocent bystander was going to be mowed down by a hail of gunfire. Once Griffin and Jason arrived, they would be headed into even more remote areas, and as this was a state with more cattle than people that was pretty fucking remote.

Logan had some sort of plan brewing in his head but Reed wasn't sure exactly what it was. Getting his old nemesis away from everybody and everything seemed to be step number one. Step two? Reed wasn't sure, but he trusted his friend not to do anything completely crazy. Logan listened to his gut and so far it hadn't been wrong, but that didn't mean it was always going to be right. There were many lives on the line here and not just the people at this camp.

The men had already decided that the women and children would sleep inside the cabin and they'd stay in the tents surrounding the area. The women, however, weren't all that appreciative of their chivalry. The twins even less so.

"I want to sleep outside in a tent," Colt whined. At this moment he looked so much like his father. "Why do I have to sleep inside the cabin? That's for girls."

"I want to camp outside too, and I'm a girl," Brianna said, her lips pressed together. She was a tiny Ava. Reed's heart squeezed tightly in his chest. He and Kaylee weren't going to experience this. Ever. Most of the time he was fine with it but every now and then it would catch him unawares. "Why can't we, Mom?"

"It's already been decided," Ava said in her best mom-tone. "Now let's get your backpacks inside."

"But we want to camp," Colt replied, clearly perplexed at the issue. "We've been camping before. Why can't we now?"

"Don't give your mother a hard time," Logan said in a sharp tone. "Remember how we talked about being helpful?"

"But—"

Ava placed her hands on her son's shoulders and dropped a kiss on the top of his head. "Colten Andrew, do not argue with your father."

A kid always knew when the shit had hit the fan and that's when mom or dad used their full name. Colt rolled his eyes but he'd given in and let it go. For now. Reed had a feeling this discussion wasn't over.

"Please take your backpacks inside the cabin," Ava commanded and the children scrambled to do her bidding. "Thank you."

Kaylee reached for the paper sacks in the back of the vehicle, but Reed shooed her away. "We've got that, honey. Why don't you and Ava get settled in the cabin?"

"Me? Why would I stay in the cabin?"

To Reed's amusement, Logan threw up his hands up in the air in frustration. "Doesn't anyone want to stay in the cabin? Shit."

Kaylee grinned and elbowed Reed. "Sorry, Logan. I just assumed I'd be sleeping out here with my husband."

Reed couldn't think of anything he'd like better, but he'd thought she'd be more comfortable in the house. The nights were cold up here in the mountains.

"Wherever you want is fine," Reed assured her. "Why don't you talk it over with Ava?"

"Men," Ava sighed, linking her arm with Kaylee's. "Let's go inside before my two lovely children have toys scattered all over. I need to freshen up as well."

"Mike, why don't you go with them?" Amy said, tapping on her phone. "Keep an eye out."

Mike headed for the weathered front door. "Will do."

It rubbed Reed the wrong way how Amy ordered Mike around and generally let him do most of the crap work. The poor guy was living like a vampire, constantly working all night on watch duty. He'd said a few words to Jared and Logan about it but they didn't want to intervene between the two marshals unless they had to. As it was, they were all walking a fine line and trying not to upset the powers-that-be in the government. Right now, everyone was friendly and cooperating and they needed it to stay that way.

Colt, Brianna, Ava, and Kaylee trailed after the marshal, leaving the men to unload the vehicles before the ice cream melted.

Amy tucked her phone in her pocket. "I sent Mike inside because I wanted to talk with you."

Chocolate mint was going to be soup very soon so this better be important.

Logan leaned a hip against the SUV. "What about?"

Amy stood up straight, her chin lifted as if she expected an argument. Depending on what she had to say, she might get one.

"I think that we need to be in a high traffic area. Lots of people. I think we should head for Salt Lake City."

Before Reed could speak Logan had abandoned his casual stance, his entire body on guard.

"Whoa, here. Salt Lake City? What makes you think we'll be safe there?"

"I second that question," Reed said. "What makes you think Salt Lake is safe? Why not stay closer to home?"

Crossing her arms over her chest, Amy cleared her throat. "A major metropolitan area is not a place that Bryson will want to be. Too many people can recognize him."

Logan snorted derisively. "Or more people for him to hurt or kill. He's not working on logic here."

"Do you want to take the chance?" Amy challenged. "We know he's watching us. He would never expect us to pick up and head for Utah."

Logan shook his head. "I don't want to be on the road that long. We're too exposed."

He was obviously thinking about when they'd all helped Evan Davis transport a prisoner headed for Florence. That hadn't gone well and had resulted in a career-ending injury for Evan.

"I think you're wrong."

They were at a stalemate. Amy completely sure and the rest

of them not sure at all.

"I'll talk to my team," Logan finally conceded. "See what they have to say. In the meantime, it's business as usual. Let's get everything unloaded and set up camp."

Whirling on the heel of her boot, Amy stomped into the cabin, apparently not happy that she hadn't been listened to.

"She's honked off," Logan observed when the front door slammed. "I don't envy Ava and Kaylee right now."

"Or Mike," Jared replied. "Seriously, what do you think about what she said?"

Not answering for a long moment, Logan finally shrugged. "Fuck, I don't know. Personally, I think that she's being a pain in the ass. What about you guys?"

Logan already knew Reed's feelings on the subject. "I am in favor of a more populated area, but I don't think we need to go as far as Salt Lake to find it. That drive sounds risky."

Jared's brows rose and he flicked a glance toward the cabin. "You know, I think she was trying to impress you, Reed. Show you what a great agent she is."

"I'm really not paying any attention. My mind is on other far more important matters."

Like Logan's issue. Like his marriage. Those two items took up all of his time.

"That's what we need to concentrate on," Logan said. "Keep our eye on the ball and not let all of these distractions get in the way."

Because Wade wouldn't let any distractions get in the way of his goals.

CHAPTER FIFTEEN

Kaylee could barely keep her eyes open. Her lids weighed about a hundred pounds and her limbs were like lead. She was lying back on Reed's chest staring at the crackling campfire while wrapped in a flannel blanket. She was cozy, warm, and her belly was full of s'mores. It was a recipe for deep sleep.

But she didn't want to go to sleep. She wanted to keep lying here with her husband and stare up at the starry night sky. The temperature had dropped sharply when the sun went down but Reed – as usual – was like a portable heater, keeping her toasty and warm along with the fire only a few feet away.

The group was circled around the campfire after putting Colt and Brianna in bed. Inside the cabin. There had been more protests and whining, but Ava had put a quick stop to all of that and tucked them in with a kiss. The men were discussing plans for the next day and Mike and Amy were patrolling the perimeter. Kaylee didn't know what had happened with the female marshal but she'd been acting rather pissed off since they'd arrived.

I hope Reed told her where to go.

"You're falling asleep."

Craning her head back, she looked up at her husband who was looking down at her. He was wearing a gentle smile and there was love in his soft golden eyes. It was moments like these that gave her hope that they could weather this horrible storm. She wanted to believe that Reed loved her more than he wanted a baby. She certainly loved him that much.

"Am not."

"Are too."

Giggling, she reached up and brushed her fingers softly across his stubbly jaw. "Maybe I am."

"Honey, you were snoring."

Uh oh. She was a snorer, thanks to a deviated septum and terrible allergies. Had everyone else heard?

Face warm, she struggled to sit up her body, not responding as quickly as it normally did. She really had been asleep. "I'm awake now."

"But not for long. You should go to bed. In the cabin."

They'd already discussed this.

"I'm fine in the tent with you. There really isn't any room for me in the cabin anyway. Ava has one bedroom and the kids have the other. Amy has the couch."

"She's not supposed to be sleeping. She's supposed to be protecting all of you."

It had been decided that Amy would take the night watch over the cabin. As for the perimeter, Reed and Logan were taking the first half and Mike and Jared would be on after one in the morning. Tomorrow Amy could sleep the day away for all anyone cared.

Glancing at the others who were deep in conversation, Kaylee kept her voice low. "I'd rather be in the tent with you. Is that alright?"

They made so much progress in the last twenty-four hours.

Kaylee didn't want to lose that. It was silly because sleeping in the cabin wouldn't make things worse between her and Reed. But it wouldn't make it any better, either. Honestly, she wanted to lie beside her husband.

"It's fine. I just want you to get a good night's sleep. I know how you struggle with that."

She did fight insomnia. Her brain was always thinking about new stories and characters and it made it hard to fall asleep. It had been extra hard without him next to her.

"I think I'll sleep. I'm tired enough."

"I'll help you to bed."

Kaylee was no lightweight but Reed lifted her to her feet as if she was a feather, tucking the blanket around her shoulders. She bid a sleepy goodnight to their friends and followed him to one of the small tents. "Actually, before I go to bed, I think I'll run into the cabin to brush my teeth. I'll change in the bathroom."

"Ah, good idea. I'll grab your bag for you." Reed ducked into the tent and came out with her cosmetics case and her pajamas. "Here you go. Is there anything else you need?"

That was a loaded question. She needed so many things but this wasn't the moment to discuss them.

"I'm good. What time will you come to bed?"

"Long after you're asleep. Don't worry about me. I don't need as much sleep as you do, remember?"

She did. He worked some terrible hours as a sheriff. Not all the time, but enough.

After a quick trip into the cabin, Kaylee snuggled down into the sleeping bag, the flannel blanket spread out over the top. Tired and worn out, she had no trouble falling asleep, but her dreams had her tossing and turning finally waking when she heard Reed creep into the tent. He was trying hard not to wake her but the tent was so small it was a losing battle.

"You can turn the light on. I'm awake," she whispered.

"I was trying not to wake you up."

Instead of the lantern, Reed turned on a small flashlight and placed it on top of his suitcase so it wouldn't shine in her eyes. Yawning, Kaylee stretched under the covers and turned onto her side. His cheeks were bright red from the cold and she had to ball her fists around the covers so she wouldn't reach out and rub them. Things had been better between them but... She still wasn't sure where they stood with each other. There was hope though, and for that she was grateful.

"I know but it's no big deal. I was having some bad dreams so I'm glad I'm awake."

Shrugging off his coat and boots, Reed frowned. "What about? Bryson?"

"I don't know what they were about specifically. I just know that I woke up tense. Is everything out there okay?"

"All quiet."

"You could sound happier about that."

"I am happy. It's just..."

His voice trailed off but Kaylee had an idea what was bothering him.

"It's too quiet?"

"Bryson is toying with us. This is the calm before the storm." Reed shucked off his pants and shirt before sliding under the covers. Immediately, she felt the warmth from his body just like the campfire earlier. "Logan is more determined than ever to send Ava and the kids down to Florida with Evan. That means you, too."

"I don't want to leave you."

The thought of Reed getting hurt and her a couple thousand miles away was unthinkable.

"A few days ago you couldn't wait to get away from me."

He'd said it with an amused tone but his statement was dead serious. And true. So much had changed in a short period of time.

"I'm trying, Reed. I'm trying hard to reach out and trust you. This isn't easy for me."

"I know and I've been thinking about that. I truly don't remember how I looked that day at the doctor's office, but I admit that the news hit me hard. We'd been trying and I guess I just thought it was only a matter of time. Miracles of medicine and all that. But I do know that I want to spend the rest of my life with you. I don't care if we ever have a child. I want to prove that to you so you can feel safe with me, honey."

Kaylee was overwhelmed that he wanted to do that, but she couldn't think of any way to make that happen overnight.

"I think it's just going to take time."

His arm slipped under her, pulling her close enough to feel his heartbeat under her ear. When they were cuddled together like this, it was as if the rest of the world didn't even exist.

"I've been thinking about that, too. You know I'm not the most patient of men."

She covered her laughter with a coughing fit. "I wouldn't necessarily say that."

"Because you're too kind. But I know how I am. I want you to be okay now, not months from now."

"I don't think that's how this works."

There was silence and for a moment Kaylee thought her exhausted husband had fallen asleep.

"When we get back home I'm going to make an appointment with Doctor Wallace and get a vasectomy."

If Kaylee hadn't been awake before, she was wide awake now. Her heart had stopped in her chest but was now beating so fast it was like she'd run a marathon.

"I don't think I heard you correctly."

She congratulated herself on her calm, cool tone when inside she was freaking out. What was Reed saying?

"You did. I'm going to get a vasectomy."

Sitting up, she tried to see her husband's face but it was shrouded in darkness. Was this some sort of cruel joke? Because it wasn't even remotely funny.

"A vasectomy? Whatever for?"

It didn't make any sense. They weren't going to have a baby so…why?

"To prove to you once and for all that I want you more than I want a baby. If I can't father a child and stay with you, I think it might help you believe me."

Her throat tight, she had to blink at the tears burning the backs of her eyes. This man. This crazy, wonderful man. He was willing to go under the knife just to prove a point to her. Something he shouldn't have to do. Was their marriage this far off the tracks? And if it was, it was certainly her fault.

"Honey, you haven't said anything for like five minutes."

Tears she couldn't hold back streamed down her cheeks. Her heart ached with love for this man.

"Because I don't know what to say. I love you so much and you're insane."

"Insane but I love him anyway or insane and what the hell am I doing married to him?"

"You know I love you," Kaylee said, her throat clogged with emotion. She could taste the salt of her tears on her lips. "I didn't think I could love you more but now I do. Isn't that crazy?"

"I think it's supposed to work like that. It's easy to be in love when everything is good. It's a hell of a lot harder for love to survive when it has to fight to stay alive."

Wrapping her arms around her torso, she shivered in the night air. "I'm so scared, and sometimes I'm not even sure what I'm frightened of."

"I'm scared, too. We can do this but we have to stick together." His hands gently pulled her back down on the air mattress so she was tucked into his side. "I love you, Kaylee Blue Mitchell. You brought me back from the dead and I can't go back to living that way again."

She understood now what Reed had gone through when they'd met. How much courage it had taken to put the past behind him and trust in a new future.

"And you returned the favor. I've only been half alive lately, too." Scrubbing at her wet cheeks with her pajama top, she snuggled closer to Reed's body heat. "We need to find a new dream. I don't know what it is but I know that we need to redefine our lives in a brand-new way."

"Whatever you want, that's what we'll do."

"I don't know what I want except for us to be together."

"I never really went away."

No, he never really had. Even when she'd ruthlessly pushed him out of her life he'd always been there. In her thoughts, and definitely in her heart.

A new dream. What would it be?

CHAPTER SIXTEEN

At lunchtime, the twins wanted to have a picnic by the lake with a blanket on the ground and all the food the ants could eat. Ava had tried to point out to both Colt and Brianna that *every* meal technically was a picnic since they were camping, but the children said it didn't count if they weren't sitting on the ground.

Which was why Kaylee was spreading out two large tarps on the lush grass close to the banks of the shimmering lake. It was a gorgeous summer day in the mountains, sunny but chilly. The men were grilling hamburgers and hot dogs while joking around about jumping into the icy water and playing polar bears. Ava had the twins "helping" by setting out the napkins, paper plates, and plastic cups on a folding table.

It might not last long, but the current vibe was one of almost-happiness. The entire camp seemed more relaxed, although the reason they were all here was still running loose.

"Need help?"

Reed knelt down and straightened a corner of the tarp so it was smooth.

"Too many men by the grill?" she teased, wanting nothing

more than to make their relationship good and happy. She was tired of being tired. And sad. And lonely. She wanted to fix her marriage, although it wasn't going to be magically healed by a night of sex and a lot of hugs. They had work ahead of them. Lots of it, but she was determined. Reed loved her, and that was something she hadn't been sure of only a few days ago.

But to be honest, she hadn't much loved herself. There had been a great deal of self-loathing going on.

"Logan and Jared have it under control." His fingers brushed hers as they laid down the second tarp. "I thought you might need a hand."

Thoughts of what those hands could do had her cheeks hot. Reed had always been able to do this to her. "Thank you. Are you hungry?"

Chit chat. Small talk. It was still hard to feel completely comfortable around him. It was almost like in the early days of their relationship.

"Starved. How about you?"

The only saving grace was that it appeared to be none too easy for him as well. Perhaps it was because they were both trying to avoid any subject that would break the harmony and cause discord.

"I could eat. The twins look excited, don't they? Ava and I have been trying to keep them occupied when you guys are discussing the real reason we're all here."

"You've been doing a great job. They think we're all on vacation and let's hope it stays that way."

Logan raised his arm and waved. "Hey everyone, just got a text from Mike. He says that Griffin and Jason have arrived."

Mike was currently on guard duty watching the entrance to the driveway along with Amy. A cheer went up at Logan's news and Jared quickly threw more food on the grill. From what

Kaylee had heard, the sheriffs would have been on the road most of the night, so they had to be tired and hungry.

Sodas were pressed into the newcomers' hands and they were ushered into a couple of folding chairs. Both men were ridiculously large for the flimsy lawn chairs and Griffin especially looked like he might break it. He was like a giant sitting in a child's chair. He was also the more talkative of the two men while Jason was far more quiet and reserved. Jason had been held hostage for months by a brutal drug cartel years ago and since then always seemed to be slightly on edge, watching his back at all times.

Jason glanced at Griffin before speaking, his phone in his hand. "Evan wants us to call him right away."

An icy cold swept over Kaylee as she closely watched the men's faces. Both Jason and Griffin appeared grim and exhausted, their demeanor tense and stiff. The way Jason had made that statement it didn't sound like it was good news.

Logan downed the last of his soda and tossed it at the large cardboard box they'd set up as a trash can. "Fuck."

It wasn't the height of eloquence but he'd certainly summed up the situation. Something bad had happened. Something worse than Wade breaking out of jail.

Who had he killed now? They'd all been expecting more deaths, but they hadn't known when. For a few hours this morning, they'd forgotten that they were waiting for the other shoe to drop.

Everyone was quiet waiting for Jason to go on. Even the birds seemed to stop singing and the wind stilled in the trees. A twig cracking could be heard a mile away.

"I'll get him on the phone and put him on speaker," Jason said, pushing a few buttons. Most phones didn't work out there, but the group was using satellite phones that should function no matter how remote the location. Kaylee's own cell didn't even have one bar here at the cabin. "We got a text from him right before we arrived here. He said it was news about Wade."

Evan's voice was soft but clear. "Hey, guys. Thanks for calling me back."

"You've got news?" Logan asked, moving closer to the phone. "About Wade?"

"Sort of about Wade. It's about him and it's also about a couple of marshals that have been working on finding him." No one said anything so Evan went on. "The SUV that the marshals were traveling in was ambushed. Two men were killed. Gunshot wounds. They found a piece of paper on the driver's seat of the car with the location of your cabin marked on a map."

Jared swore under his breath as Logan turned his back and stared out at the calm waters of the lake. Reed grabbed Kaylee's hand and squeezed.

"There is good news," Evan said.

Logan snorted and whirled around. "Shit, we could use some about now. What's the good news?"

"One of the marshals got off a call before he was killed. There were at least three men that ambushed them. Turner identified Wade but he didn't know the other two. There might have been additional backup but he didn't see them. So now we know that Wade is in the area and that he has the help of at least two men. That's more than we knew before."

"Wade's a complete psychopath," Reed growled. "What does he get from killing those men?"

Kaylee placed another hand on top of her husband's in what she hoped was a soothing action.

"Wade wants to torture me," Logan replied, his lips a flat line. "He wants me to worry about everybody else when I should be worried about what he's going to do."

Logan had said out loud the words they'd all been thinking.

"He wants to win the game," Logan said.

Kaylee shivered at the expression on his face. Remote and icy. Dangerous. She'd seen that same look on Reed's face and she'd always feared it. When the men were like this, they couldn't be swayed from whatever they were planning.

"We're not going to let him," Evan declared. "I already called Tanner and Seth and they're on their way to the site of the ambush to see if they can find any clues as to where they might have gone off to. In the meantime, I'm still digging as to who might be helping Bryson. If we can find them, we might be able to find him."

Ava's gaze ran from her husband to Jared to Reed and then back again. "So what do we do now?"

Kaylee had been wondering that very thing. From the look on Logan's face, they weren't going to like the answer.

Ava managed to drag Logan into the cabin without garnering the attention of her two children who were playing kickball with Kaylee and Reed. Her husband had that look on his face, and she knew quite well what it meant.

He wanted to go after Wade Bryson.

If she were honest with herself, she'd known this was coming. With every passing hour that Wade wasn't found, they ticked closer to this outcome. Logan was a man on a mission and that mission had just killed two more people. It wasn't in his DNA to sit around and hope things all worked out. He was a man of action and staying still like this went against every instinct inside of him.

Which was why it was going to be damn difficult to get him to see reason.

"We need to talk about this."

Slamming his fist down on the kitchen counter, Logan's jaw tightened. "This isn't the time, babe."

"This is the time. I know what you're thinking and you need to put it out of your mind. You can't do it."

It was a mistake to draw the line so bluntly. Logan didn't like being challenged and if she'd been thinking straight she wouldn't have done it but dammit, she was emotional, too. This was her life and her children and all she wanted to do was go home. She'd hoped this would only be a few days but it was stretching on longer than either one of them had ever imagined.

"Don't tell me what to do."

Snorting, Ava rolled her eyes. "As if you'd ever listen. You're as ornery as a mule and twice as stubborn. I knew that when I met you and I knew it even more when I married you, but I never thought you'd be stupid."

"I'm not stupid," Logan growled, that muscle in his jaw working overtime. If the red color on his neck was anything to go by, she'd hit a nerve. That was good. He needed a dose of truth right about now.

"No, you're smart. Most of the time, but at this moment you're not thinking straight. Wade wants you to come after him. You'd be playing right into his hands."

"I know that," Logan scoffed. "But that doesn't mean I have to play his game. Can't you see that as long as we sit here scared and frightened he's in control? At least if I'm out there, I'm in control."

"I don't see it that way at all," Ava argued. "If you're doing what he wants you to, how can you be the one in control of the situation? By defying Wade, you're pissing him off and the madder he gets—"

"The more people he kills," Logan finished for her.

"I was going to say that the madder he gets, the more mistakes he'll make."

"That too." Logan sat down heavily into a kitchen chair. "But how many have to die before that happens? How many is too many?"

The lives were weighing on her husband. He took far too much on his broad shoulders. She walked behind him and placed her hands on the top of his head, her fingers brushing the short but silky strands before rubbing his temples.

"Even one is too many but you're not responsible for all of this. Wade is. He's the one making those choices, not you."

"Wade is a fucking sociopath."

"Yes, and you're the sane one here, and you have to know that going after him is walking right into a trap."

His head fell back, his eyes closed. "I can't sit around here with my thumb up my ass. I can't sit here and let him kill more innocent people. We have to find him sooner rather than later."

"And the marshal service has people trying to do just that."

Ava wanted to believe that but her voice wavered when she said it. If the government could find Wade, they'd already have him behind bars.

Logan laughed, but not because it was funny. It was actually the opposite. "Give me twenty-four hours in the field and I could find him and bring him in."

"Is that a request, cowboy?"

His eyes opened, the usually warm blue almost gray with his stormy emotions. He was gazing directly at her, looking right into her heart and soul. "Yes."

"We said we would put the family first. Our children, Logan."

He sat up and spun around, linking his arms around her waist. "I've thought about that. You, Kaylee, and the twins…

You go to Florida where Evan can watch over you. I know you'll be safe there. Wade can't get that far."

Logan had wanted to send them to Florida first thing and she'd convinced him not to, certain that once they were out of the way he'd go after Wade on his own. But now…he might have a point. She'd wanted to stay with Logan but she had to put the kids first. Logan was resourceful and a hell of a lawman. He could take care of himself.

I have to believe that.

"Talk to your friends," she finally conceded. "Talk to them and get their input. If they agree that it's time to go after him, I won't argue. Kaylee and I will take the kids to Florida and wait this out."

Her husband, bless him, didn't appear to believe her. He was no dummy but this time she wasn't kidding.

"Really? You'll go? No fighting about it?"

"No fighting. Heck, maybe we'll even go to Disney World. Seth and Presley had a good time there when she was on the run."

It was a feeble attempt at a joke and her husband didn't laugh or smile.

"That's…good, then."

Leaning down, she pressed a soft kiss against his lips. A tingle ran through her and she marveled that this man could still rock her world two kids and a myriad of years later. Especially when they had about a hundred other things going on.

"I trust you." *I will. I have to.* "But if you end up dead, I'll kill you."

Smiling, Logan stood and pulled her even closer to his solid, muscular frame. She couldn't imagine him not in her life. It scared her to even think about it. Kaylee and Reed's issues had put the fear into Ava. No one's marriage was immune to trouble.

No matter how good things are going, they can always get fucked up.

"Fair enough, babe. But I don't plan on gettin' dead."

It was the unplanned actions she was worried about.

CHAPTER SEVENTEEN

"Wade can't stay out there forever. We'll get him."

That assurance had come from Jason, who clearly wasn't fond of Logan's idea to stop playing defense and go after the escaped killer. He'd pulled his friends into the cabin to talk while the kids played outside. Griffin had stayed with Ava and Kaylee to help guard them.

"We haven't gotten him so far," Logan argued. "I think I could be more useful in the field than stuck in a safe house which, by the way, we don't have because Wade knows were we are. He's going to keep killing and I have to stop him."

Evan was working to find them another safe house somewhere near but not too close to this one.

"You or us?" Jared asked. "Because I thought we were a team."

"We are a team," Logan replied. "I couldn't do this without you guys, but when it all comes down to it this has turned personal for me."

Jason blew out a noisy breath. "When I hear you say that I know that we're in trouble. You have to keep a cool head, my friend, or you're going to get yourself killed. Or one of us. I got to tell you that I'm not ready to die. I have a lot to live for."

"So do I and that's why I can't let Wade run around free. The longer we go without catching him, the more confident he's going to get. I don't think that's a good thing."

"It might be," Jared argued. "It might make him sloppy. He'll make a mistake and we'll get him."

"He hasn't made any mistakes so far and I'm growing old waiting for it. He's come after the marshals. It's only a matter of time before he comes after one of you or maybe my family. He wants to get to me, hurt me before he kills me, and the more he tortures me the better. May I remind you that he was going to slice me up and watch me bleed to death slowly?"

Logan remembered that fucking day as if it were yesterday. Bright, Technicolor memories that would be with him for the rest of his life. Not so much from the danger – Logan hadn't ever really felt that he was going to die – but the horrifying realization that Wade was the vigilante killer. That had been the awful part.

"We remember," Jason said grimly. "We know what he's capable of. I'm just not sure that going after him is the right move. He's trying to lure you out into the open."

"He's doing a good job of it."

Jared tapped the table to emphasize his point. "Our job is to keep you and your family under wraps and safe."

Logan shrugged. "Plans change. They need to be fluid. I'm not asking permission here, if that's what you're thinking. If I think that the best thing to do is go after Wade, then that's what I'm going to do."

He didn't mention his conversation with Ava and how she'd wanted his friends' buy-in to the whole scheme.

"You're a grown man and you don't need our permission, but you might need our help," Jason pointed out. "I'm not letting you go after Wade Bryson all alone. I'll shoot you myself before I let you do that."

Logan didn't doubt Jason's vow and for a moment an image of himself limping around camp because Jason shot him in the leg came to mind.

"I'd still go after Wade." Logan's gaze veered over to the man sitting on the couch, his feet propped up on the old coffee table. Reed hadn't said a damn word since they'd come in to talk about this. "What about you, Mitchell? What do you think?"

Taking a drink of his coffee, Reed seemed to consider his words before answering. "I think that Logan is right."

Stunned silence. Logan was surprised at the vote of confidence and Jared and Jason looked shocked as well.

"Of course, I'm right," Logan finally replied. "We can't sit around and wait for Wade to move. We need to do something."

Reed smiled and raised his hand in a stop motion. "Whoa. I said that I agreed. Up to a point. We do need to do something. Clearly, this isn't working and you know what they say about the definition of insanity. I don't want to keep making the same mistake and expecting a different outcome. We need to make a change, but I think we need to think about what that change actually is very fucking carefully."

It was the closest thing to an endorsement that Logan was going to get. He'd take it.

"So we need a new plan."

"Yes," Reed agreed. "And the first thing we need to do is get the women and children out of the way. With them here, we're constantly worrying about them. Get Evan on the phone and let's put them on a plane south as soon as possible."

Logan couldn't agree more. "That's what I wanted to do originally but Ava wasn't going for it. And honestly, I wanted to keep them close."

"That's normal," Jason said. "After all, no one can keep them as safe as their husband and father can, but right now you're the lightning rod in all of this. They're better off away from you. But will Ava agree to it?"

"If you all agree, she said she'd go." Logan turned to Reed. "What about Kaylee? She'll want to stay with you."

Logan didn't know what was going on with his friend's marriage, but something was definitely wrong. The tension lessened in the last few days, however, and it might be a task to get Kaylee to leave Reed just when things were getting better.

"She'll go," Reed said, his expression determined. "If I have to put her on that plane myself, she'll go."

"So we all agree?" Logan looked around at his friends. "A new plan? A new start?"

The three other men nodded, although they didn't look all that happy. Too bad.

Already Logan felt like a new person. He hated sitting around waiting for Wade.

"We need to get Bryson reacting to us instead of the other way around. He's not so smart when he doesn't have time to think things through. We need him making split-second decisions. That's when he's going to do something stupid and then we'll get him."

Because failure wasn't an option.

Reed placed Kaylee's suitcase in the back of their vehicle. "Don't worry. It's not a long drive to the new safe house Evan found for us."

The new house was closer to Denver where Ava, Kaylee, and the twins were going to board a plane tomorrow for Florida. They'd discussed having them fly out of Bozeman but they'd all felt that it would be the first place Wade would look for them. But of course, Kaylee didn't know about any of this.

Reed and his friends had spent the better part of the afternoon strategizing, discarding one plan after another until they had something they could live with. Not be happy about necessarily. But live with. Because they all wanted to stay alive.

"I'm not worried about that," Kaylee replied. "I'm worried about you. You look worried so now I worry."

Shit, do I really?

Trying to set his wife's mind at ease, he mustered a teasing smile. "Maybe I'm worried about interest rates or the price of gas."

"You never worry about those things." Kaylee stepped closer and placed her hand on his arm. She kept her voice low so he could barely hear. "Spill it. Something is going on."

Something *was* going on. Had Logan told Ava yet? There was no indication but a hell of a lot of decisions had been made in the last several hours and as usual the women were going to be the last to know.

They were all leaving under the cover of darkness and Ava and Kaylee – bless them – had barely even asked a question. They'd simply nodded and went to pack up the cabin. Reed could only hope that they'd made the right call to wait until after sundown to get on the road. It could be the correct decision or so very, very wrong.

That's why Reed looked so damn worried.

"I was going to tell you while we were on the road."

"Why don't you tell me now. Is it that bad? Has Wade done something else?"

"No, it's not that. We…"

"We?" she prompted. "Just spit it out or let me guess. We're going to Florida, right?"

She was partially correct.

"You're going to Florida. I'm staying here. In the morning. Evan is getting a private plane. He has a rich as shit friend, I guess."

To his relief, she didn't look surprised in the least. He had a feeling that she and Ava had been talking about this very thing while the men were making new plans.

"Okay, I can't say that I'm shocked. Is Wade closing in?"

"Well...yes and no. He's out there and he knows our location, but he doesn't seem to be coming after us. He's playing his game. But eventually..."

He didn't put words to the actual fears in his heart that she, Ava, or the twins might be hurt or killed because of Wade Bryson and Reed's involvement.

"How long can this go on?" she asked. "You all have jobs. I don't mean you, of course. You have more vacation saved up than any human being on the planet, but the others might actually lose their jobs."

Since meeting and marrying Kaylee, Reed had been making an effort to use up all of his saved vacation and sick days but when a person hoards them as badly as he had for years it wasn't easy. He still had two months in the bank.

He'd been hoping to use it when they had a baby. Now they'd need to find another reason. Maybe when this was all over, he could sweep her off her feet and take her on a long second honeymoon. They'd been talking about traveling someday. That day might be soon.

"If they get fired Jason, Jared, and Logan will simply hire them for the consulting firm. They're busier than hell apparently and they want to start a new division that would specialize in bigger, more complex cases."

"You'd be good at that."

Reed hadn't considered himself for the team. He had a town to run and people that depended on him.

"All the guys would. So are you ready to get on the road?"

"Let's do this."

He could only hope and pray that she had no idea just how dangerous what they were about to do truly was. This wasn't going to be a fun little road trip. Wade Bryson and his henchmen might be out there waiting for them.

CHAPTER EIGHTEEN

Reed's fingers gripped the steering wheel, his knuckles white and his palms sweaty. Outwardly he hoped he conveyed a sense of ease and calm, but inside his guts were churning and he could taste the acid in the back of his throat. There was a real fear that Bryson was watching and might ambush them just as he had done with the marshals.

To protect the women and children, he and his friends had put them in the middle of their small convoy. He'd persuaded Kaylee to ride with Logan, Ava, and the twins and they were currently in the minivan right in front of him. Griffin sat in Reed's passenger seat while Jason and Jared led the group in their vehicle with Amy and Mike right behind.

Tanner and Seth were planning to meet them at the new safe house. With any luck, they'd all arrive safe and alive.

Funny how the drive to the cabin in the daytime hadn't been this nerve-wracking, but then Bryson's body count had been lower. The psychopath was determined to fuck with Logan before killing him in some strange "clean up the Bryson family name" vendetta. Logan didn't even use the Bryson name and he was a damn fine upstanding citizen. As far as Reed was concerned, that looney tune was using it all as an excuse to kill. Because he fucking enjoyed it, the bastard. Wade Bryson got his jollies killing people. End of story. He also knew he was never going to be as good as Logan, so he'd decided to wipe him off the face of the earth.

Reed and his friends weren't about to let that happen.

That meant they had to make this drive without anyone getting killed or injured. There weren't any streetlights out this far and it was as dark as the devil's asshole out here. They'd made the decision to keep their headlights off, so that meant that they had to keep their speed down since no one could see a goddamn thing. They were literally traveling by the light of the moon and their satellite navigation systems. Thank heaven it was a clear night.

The only good news was that if they couldn't see anything, then neither could Bryson and whomever was helping him.

They only had to do this for a little while longer and then they'd be out in the open on a major highway. They'd gone back and forth for awhile about whether they should stick to the side roads but had finally decided that Bryson wouldn't want to be anywhere around large numbers of people. That was another reason they'd chosen the Denver area.

Griffin shifted in his seat, craning his neck to see in the darkness. "Jesus, I never realized just how dark it gets away from the city lights. It's like driving through black ink."

Sweat trickling down Reed's back, he could only nod in agreement. The heater blasted hot air into the vehicle and he would have reached over to turn it down, but he didn't want to take his eyes from the road for a second. He couldn't see the damn knob anyway, so he'd just have to sweat. Assuming it was the temperature making him sweat and not the stress.

While Reed drove, Griffin was supposed to keep his eyes

peeled for anything out of the ordinary and that meant anything literally. Animals, cars, unexplained lights. Whatever might be a threat to their safety. The silence stretched on as the minutes ticked slowly by, each one taking them closer to civilization. Reed wasn't sure whether he would be relieved or even more wary. Complacency was the enemy.

"Jason said that you were the one that swayed the vote on going after Bryson."

The road was becoming less twisty and Reed's tension had lowered a notch or two. His fingers loosened on the steering wheel and he brought his right hand down to dry the damp palm on his jeans.

"I guess," Reed finally replied. "As I said it's crazy to keep doing the same thing and just hoping shit gets better. It's not getting better, it's only getting worse."

"He's taking this too personally. He's too emotional and he's going to get someone killed."

Him being Logan.

"Maybe," Reed conceded. "I have to say though I've seen Logan go cold as ice in certain situations. He's not a hothead. But yeah, this situation is a cluster of mammoth proportions and he's at the center of it all. And that's personal. I don't see how it can't be personal. This is about Bryson and Logan. And in the end, it's going to be between the two of them. When the time comes, let him take the shot. Fuck, he's earned it."

"Has it already been decided? Bryson's not going back to prison?"

There was no censure in Griffin's tone. None at all.

"No, but you know how accurate Logan's gut is?" Griffin nodded in the darkness. "Well, his gut is telling him that Bryson isn't going back to prison. It's going to be dead or alive and only one of them walks away. Or maybe he's watched too many

Charles Bronson movies. Either way, I don't think this guy is going to just throw up his hands and surrender. He doesn't want to go back and be a guest of the state and he has to know that this time he'll go to Florence. I'm guessing he'd rather go to hell than a Supermax."

"And Bryson will take out anyone in his way."

Was that what this was about?

"He will. Are you worried? You don't have to do this, you know. We can get you on the plane and you can watch over the women and kids. No one would question you."

"That's not it. I just can't help but wonder…" Griffin paused as if gathering his thoughts. "What makes a person go so far to the other side? What sent this guy on a one-way trip to suicide by cop?"

"He did see his father murder his mother," Reed reminded his friend. "And God knows what else. I don't know enough about sociopaths to know whether they're born or made. Maybe a little of both. Logan says that Bryson wants to go out in a blaze of glory. He wants news coverage, headlines, and books written about him."

"That's sick as shit."

"Damn right. I'm making it my personal mission to make sure that he doesn't become famous. The day after we capture him I want him to be completely forgotten by the public. No books. No movies. No groupies. Lock him up and throw away the key. He can never be rehabilitated."

"This has to be driving Logan out of his mind. The rising body count has to be making him crazy."

"It is," Reed confirmed. "Frankly, I'm surprised we were able to keep him in check this long. He won't be happy until he's put an end to Bryson's reign of terror."

The crackling of the radio captured their attention as Jared announced that they were taking the next exit to the main highway. They would begin seeing other vehicles in a few minutes.

Stay alert and vigilant.

Kaylee was beginning to lose count as to how many times she'd packed and re-packed her suitcase. They were in another house, this time in an affluent suburb outside of Boulder. They'd arrived in the middle of the night like thieves, sneaking out of their camp and into this home.

She'd barely noticed it last night, intent on getting the twins settled into bed and making sandwiches for the hungry men, but it was quite lovely. High ceilings, oak floors, and large airy rooms. The home was surrounded by tall trees which would block anyone's view into the windows, which she assumed was by design. Did these innocent suburbanites realize that the United States government owned this home and kept key witnesses under cover here? Probably not.

After getting a bite to eat, she'd eventually fallen into a deep sleep despite all the caffeine she'd ingested that evening, but it hadn't been restorative in the least. She was just as tired as when she went to bed. This situation was starting to wear on her and she could only imagine how Ava and Logan felt. She'd crawled out of bed this morning and taken a shower but now standing in front of the bathroom mirror wrapped in a towel she barely had the energy to put on a coat of mascara.

I'm only going on an airplane. Does anyone really care how I look?

"Hey, babe."

Reed stuck his head around the doorway, his face covered in stubble and his hair askew from running his fingers through it. If he'd come to bed at any time last night, she hadn't stirred. More likely, he and the others had stayed up talking about plans and strategy. His eyes were slightly red-rimmed and he looked…exhausted. He needed about a week of sleep. They all did really, but that wasn't in the cards.

"Hey. I don't suppose you got any sleep last night?"

Shaking his head, he stepped into the steamy bathroom. "I'll try and catch a nap after we take you to the airport. Josie and Evan are meeting us there which is outstanding news. You'll be even more protected on the flight down."

Evan, of course, was a former US Marshal and Josie was no slouch either. When she'd met Evan, she'd been on the run for a crime she didn't commit. Smart and resourceful, she had successfully dodged the bad guys after her all on her own until Evan had stepped in to help.

"That's really nice of them. I thought we'd just meet them in Florida." She scraped her wet hair away from her face. "I was just trying to figure out if I needed to put any makeup on."

"You don't need it."

Checking out her pale face in the mirror, she stuck out her tongue at the reflection. "Men always say that but it's not really true. I need makeup but I'm too tired to apply it."

Slowly, as if she might push him away, Reed slid his arms around her, pulling her close despite the damp towel she was wearing. He was going to get his clothes wet. "It's true. You don't need it. You're beautiful just the way you are. Drop dead gorgeous."

Only a man in love could say those things and actually look like he truly meant it. Her insides melted into goo and she rested her head against his chest, the steady thump of his own heart under her cheek.

"You're wrong but I love hearing that kind of stuff."

"I'm not wrong. You're just hard on yourself."

That seemed to be a trend. After talking to Ava, she was trying hard to be kinder to herself but habits die hard.

"I'm going to miss you."

His strong hands ran up and down her back, dislodging the towel so that it fell to the floor. His rough fingertips glided down her spine and she couldn't help her shiver in response. It felt so amazing to be touched and cuddled. She'd missed this so much.

"I'll miss you too, but this will all be over before you know it. Then I promise you we'll make a new start."

"You didn't expect it to go on this long."

"That's true but this time Logan is going after Bryson personally. It won't be long now."

Her arms tightened around his lean middle and she took a lungful of his delicious scent so she could hold onto it while they were apart. "Promise me you'll be careful. That you won't take any stupid chances."

Reed was the quintessential man's man with complete and utter self-confidence when it came to law enforcement. Luckily, he had the skills to back up that confidence but it didn't make the worry gnawing at her stomach go away.

He leaned back, his hand cupping her chin so she had to look up into his eyes. "You're not going to lose me. I'm going to dog your heels forever."

She'd be happy if that were true, but Wade Bryson had left a trail of bodies in his wake.

"Bryson is a cold-blooded killer."

"He's not the first I've gone after."

"True, but he's desperate, Reed, and he doesn't care what he does or who he hurts. He's not your average criminal."

"We'll work as a team. They've got my back and I've got theirs."

Kaylee trusted these men, but she couldn't shake the sense

of foreboding that had come over her. She wanted to hold on to Reed and never let go.

"I know. I just worry. I don't want anything to happen to you or anyone else, for that matter. If I lost you now—"

Emotion tightened her throat and she couldn't finish what she was going to say. She was basically sending her husband off to battle and that wasn't an action to be taken lightly.

His fingers stroked her cheek and his thumb slipped over her lips before he bent his head and kissed her, slow and soft at first, but then that familiar passion flared and the kiss became something far more. More eager, more passionate, and definitely more promise. This was the absolute worst moment and they didn't have time, but Kaylee needed to be close to Reed. As close as possible.

Reed pulled back reluctantly but his hands didn't stop caressing her skin. "We don't have time."

She frantically tugged at the bottom of his t-shirt, desperate to be with him one more time. "Then you'd better hurry."

Reed seemed to pick up on her urgency, stripping off his t-shirt so her hands could roam all over his tanned skin. As always, she was endlessly fascinated by his body, so hard and different from her own. Her fingers traced the ridges of his abdomen as he pulled her closer for another kiss, their tongues playing a heated game of tag.

They shouldn't be doing this and they didn't have time but dammit, they were going to get it done. Underneath the worn denim he was hard and ready, so she traced the outline of his cock, drawing a groan from his lips.

Lifting her off of the ground, he settled her onto the vanity, pressing her knees apart while kissing a wet trail down the middle of her body. What was he doing?

"We don't have time for that."

He looked up from where his mouth hovered over her mound, a smile playing on his lips.

"There's always time, baby. Sit back and let me drive."

There was nothing Reed loved more than being in control when it came to sex. Most of the time Kaylee was happy for him to take the lead, but every now and then she wanted to be in charge, too.

Now was not one of those times. She was happy for Reed to run the show.

The first touch of his tongue had her arching and twisting underneath him, but his hands on her hips held her firmly in his grasp. She was helpless as he placed her legs over his shoulders and his mouth did magic things, making her blood sizzle and flames to lick at her veins. Her head fell back onto the mirror but she barely noticed as her arousal built quickly. He wasn't teasing her as he normally did. Reed Mitchell had gone in for the kill and damn if he wasn't going to send her over practically in seconds.

The steam in the bathroom drifted around them, the heat almost consuming Kaylee as her body exploded in a series of waves that had her trembling and digging her nails into Reed's shoulders. She'd barely caught her breath when she heard the metallic sound of his zipper and then a string of curse words as he tried to free his cock. There was no sweet nothings or buildup. She was wet and ready and he plunged in deep. Kaylee cried out at the invasion but not from pain. It was like being bathed in a pool of infinite pleasure, the water gushing over her as he rode her hard and fast.

They were both breathing heavy and ragged as the pressure began to build toward another climax. Reed knew her so well, their bodies completely in tune with one another. He knew exactly what to do to send her over the edge, his cock unerringly finding that sweet spot inside of her. He ran over it time after time, pushing himself closer to the cliff as well. When they both fell over, they held each other close for the entire drop to earth. Kaylee clutched Reed, her legs wrapped around his waist and her arms around his neck, holding on for dear life.

It was quick, hot, dirty, and exactly what she needed before boarding a plane to Florida. He held her for a little while but not nearly as long as she would have liked. The world outside of these walls called to both of them. They had business and commitments. Places to be and people to protect.

Wade Bryson was still out there and until he was captured, there would be no rest.

CHAPTER NINETEEN

Ava was loading the twins into the minivan when Reed strode up to her husband, his expression grim. More bad news? It was beginning to come faster than she could process it. She quickly closed the van door so Colt and Brianna couldn't hear what their uncle was about to say.

"Amy and Mike are missing."

Reed's flat tone belied the seriousness of the words he spoke. The color that drained from Logan's face matched the rest of the men. They were all taken aback by the news, but Ava was shocked at how numb she was becoming when hearing about the evil that Wade wrought over the planet. Perhaps it was a coping mechanism, but it was like she was standing outside her body and watching the whole scene as if it was a bad television show and she needed to change the channel. If she gave into all the emotions inside of her she might not be able to do all the things she needed to.

So she'd just shut them down.

"They were watching the perimeter while we packed," Logan said, his gaze running over the assembled group. "When was the last time you saw or heard from them?"

Jared stepped forward. "I was watching the east and Amy the west. It was all good until about ten minutes ago. She didn't answer on the radio, so I called Reed to take a look in case she'd been hurt."

Nodding to Griffin beside him, Reed pointed out to the tree line. "Then I couldn't get Mike on the phone, either. We looked for them but all we found was this."

Amy's badge.

"Fuck," Logan spat out. "Wade playing more of his games."

"He couldn't have gotten far," Jared said. "We have to go after him."

"We have to get to the airfield," Griffin argued. "Tanner and Seth are meeting us there along with Evan. Then we can go after Bryson. There are only a few roads out of here. He's finally tipped his hand. We've got him."

Everyone was looking at Logan to make the call but instead Jason spoke up.

"The women and children need to get to their flight," he said, stepping into the center of the group. "That has to be our priority. They're going to need our protection on the drive to the airfield."

Rubbing his chin, Logan nodded in agreement. "You're right, and let's be sharp. If Wade is around, he may not be done playing pranks. He might be waiting for us on the road."

Logan and Reed rode in the van with Ava, Kaylee, and the twins while Griffin took his place in front with Jason and Jared in the rear. This time the drive was quite different, though. No darkness, no worrying about stealth. The sun was up and there was no hiding. This trip would be taken at maximum speed. The sooner they were on the plane, the better.

Kaylee leaned close to Ava. "I can't believe that Evan knows someone with a private plane. He's rubbing elbows with millionaires down there in Florida."

Ava chuckled. "It's Steve's plane."

Steve was their mutual friend who wrote thrillers. They'd all hung out together at a book convention years ago and drank way too much tequila. An outsider looking at Steve would think that he was a vagrant by the way he dressed and rarely combed his hair, but he was simply a little eccentric.

"Steve? Wow, I didn't realize he'd sold that many books."

"Family money," Ava replied promptly. "His parents are loaded. Like the jet set kind of loaded. He needn't work another day in his life. He just loves writing."

"Remind me to send him some candy as a thank you."

And Steve loved sugar. Any form. The man had a seriously wicked sweet tooth.

"We both will."

The rest of the journey passed uneventfully and as they grew closer to the airfield Ava could see a small jet out of the window preparing to land. They'd timed it perfectly.

"Looks like Evan and Josie made it right on time," Logan said, giving Ava an encouraging smile. This separation wasn't easy for either of them, but it had come to the point where it was better for her and the twins to be out of his way. He couldn't worry about them and do his job at the same time. But leaving him was still hard. Somehow, she felt better when he was close at hand. She had a great deal of waiting and wondering ahead of her. Luckily, Kaylee would be right there with her. This had to be difficult for her, too. "The jet stopped in Denver to fuel up so they're ready to just get you guys on board and turn around. Kids, are you excited to see Uncle Evan and Aunt Josie?"

"Mickey Mouse," Brianna called out with a grin, raising her arms triumphantly in the air. "I wanna go see Mickey."

"I want to go to the beach," Colt said, his own face lit up with glee.

Ava's heart lurched in her chest at her children's infectious happiness. They'd taken to all of this like the troopers they were. They had to know something was up, but they'd dealt with it by concentrating on the positive side of the situation.

Disney and the beach. It was a pretty terrific combination.

"We'll see about Disney and the beach," Ava said, using her best mommy tone. According to Logan, they'd be safe as kittens down there so they could move about as they pleased. "I better see some excellent behavior from you two."

"I think they'll both be eating their vegetables at dinner tonight," Kaylee said with a smile. "They're highly motivated."

"It's the only way. They're great negotiators. They have a future in used car sales."

The van came to a halt and Logan and Reed quickly climbed out along with Griffin and Jared in the other vehicle. All of the men were on high alert, scanning the area but it appeared completely deserted. Just as they'd hoped.

Reed slid open the door of the van as Logan began to unload the luggage in the back. They hadn't brought much with them. The door to the jet opened and the stairs descended followed by Josie and Evan bounding toward them with their arms outstretched. Both Colt and Brianna ran straight for the aunt and uncle, squealing with delight as only a child can. They launched themselves straight into Evan and Josie chattering about Mickey Mouse, the beach, and cheeseburgers. Ava wasn't sure what that last part was about but if her two children wanted cheeseburgers for dinner tonight she'd gladly make or buy them.

Hugs all around and Ava couldn't help the tears that welled up in her eyes at seeing their friends all come to their aid. There was something about this circle of people, so loyal and devoted.

They were all risking their lives and poor Evan was still recovering from having his appendix out. His inability to be right in the action was driving him crazy but coming to their rescue with this plane was nothing short of heroic.

Josie hugged Ava again. "Don't worry about anything. We brought all sorts of games and toys to keep the twins occupied."

She'd said the magic words. Colt and Brianna's ears perked up and their eyes widened.

"Games?" Brianna asked.

"Toys?" Colt parroted.

"Absolutely," Josie replied, rubbing her hands together. "Let's see...I think we have Uno, Hungry Hippos, Operation, and um...oh yeah, Sorry. We also brought some Legos and a few Barbies, and I think there's a whole bucket of miniature chocolate bars."

The truly magical word. Chocolate. Colt and Brianna were dancing around like it was Christmas morning. From the sounds of it, it kind of was. Christmas in July, anyway.

"But only if your mother says it's okay," Josie warned. "She's the boss."

Ha ha. Wait until Josie had her own kids. She'd be laughing about that statement someday.

Colt pointed to the plane. "Are we really going to be the only ones on the airplane?"

"We really are," Evan confirmed. "It's a private plane owned by a friend of mine and your mother's."

"Cool," Colt said, obviously straining at the bit to get on board. "Can we look inside?"

It wouldn't be a terrible thing for the kids to be onboard when Ava said goodbye to their father.

"Okay, but first give your dad a hug and tell him you love him. We're not going to see him for a few days."

Ava's eyes welled up with more tears as Logan knelt down to hug and kiss the twins. Her husband had hugged the children hundreds of times but today he held them just a second or two longer and her heart almost couldn't take it. Logan's own eyes were bright as well and he kept clearing his throat as he told them to behave and listen to their mother. He'd see them soon.

Ava desperately hoped that was true. She was counting on forever with this man. He'd promised it and she was going to hold him to it.

As soon as Logan stood, Colt and Brianna bolted for the small staircase, Josie on their heels to show them around.

"I'll take good care of them," Evan promised Logan. "Don't worry. I've got some volunteers down there to help me. Good guys that I trust absolutely. They'll be fine."

Logan's smile had disappeared and his expression had turned somber. "I trust you. This is the right thing to do."

Evan's gaze landed on Ava and then Kaylee, who was standing next to Reed. "I'll give you ladies a few moments to say goodbye. We'll wait in the jet."

The other men tried to pretend they weren't standing there too, looking in any other direction. Ava grabbed the front of Logan's t-shirt and tugged him closer.

"Be careful out there, cowboy. You have a family to come home to."

"And Mickey Mouse. Let's not forget him. When this is over, we'll have a real vacation."

Ava didn't want her husband to think that the kids were happy to leave him.

"They're just excited. The private plane and the toys and candy. In about an hour they're going to want to call you because they miss you."

"I know." Logan paused as if trying to find the right words.

"You'll be safe. I should have done this at the beginning."

"I wouldn't have gone in the beginning."

"You would have if I said that's the only way to keep the twins safe."

True, but she wouldn't have made it easy on him.

"I'll miss you," he said, leaning down to press a kiss against her lips. He wasn't one for public displays and honestly neither was she. They'd already said goodbye in private before they'd left the safe house. "Be good."

That made her laugh. "Be good? What do you think I'm going to do? Stay up past my bedtime and eat too much sugar?"

"When you and Kaylee are together, anything can happen. Seriously, I'll call you when I can."

They'd already discussed that she couldn't call him unless it was an emergency. He couldn't be sneaking up on Wade and have his phone go off.

"I know. We'll be fine. The kids are going to have fun."

"So...don't do anything stupid."

"That takes in a lot of territory, good girl. Can you be more specific?"

Good girl. It never ceased to make her warm and happy. He knew it, too. How could she be this happy when her heart was breaking all at the same time?

I'm going to see him in a few days. Alive and well. Nothing bad is going to happen. I have to believe that to even begin to get through this day.

"Specifically? Stay alive." She poked his chest with her finger. "I've got plans for you when this is all done."

"Baby, I have plans for you, too. And I told you before, I don't plan on getting dead. I underestimated Wade before but I'm not about to do it again. I've done nothing but study him and I've got his number. I know how he thinks."

Ava hoped so. Logan was probably the best lawman she'd

ever seen – along with his friends – but Wade didn't play by any rules.

Wrapping her arms around her husband, she hugged him tightly again, breathing in deeply to fill her lungs with his calming scent. One more time.

"I guess it's time–"

Ava didn't get to finish her sentence.

Because that's when the first shot rang out.

Logan shoved Ava to the ground, covering her body with his while pulling his gun from his shoulder holster. All the men had their weapons and had instinctively formed a circle around Ava and Kaylee as the bullets flew all around them.

His ears ringing from the sound of gunfire, he didn't even let himself have a second thought about his next decision. He needed to keep his children safe. They couldn't be in the middle of a firefight. This was his worst fucking nightmare and a scenario that had kept him awake several nights in a row. Waving to Evan who was now standing in the doorway of the jet, Logan called out to him.

"Go! Get out of here. Go now!"

Evan yelled something but Logan couldn't hear him. The jet engine's revved, the staircase folded up, and the door closed as the aircraft began to taxi down the runway. Ava screamed and tried to crawl toward the departing plane, but Logan wrapped his arms around her and pulled her back against the side of the van. Her nails raked at the bare flesh of his arms as she kicked and yelled, fighting him so she could chase the aircraft. He held her down until the plane lifted into the blue sky, gracefully gaining altitude and heading far away from the mayhem on the ground.

Tears were streaming down his wife's cheeks and Logan

could only hold her tighter, rocking her as she sobbed.

"My babies, my babies."

Yes, he was the SOB that had separated her from her babies. But he'd done it to keep them safe. If he'd been able to get Ava on that plane despite the gunfire, he would have put her on it, too. That had been the whole point of this exercise.

At least Colt and Brianna were protected. Safe with Evan and Josie.

"They're safe, good girl. They're safe. They're with our friends and they'd die to protect our children."

As quick as a whip, Ava turned from being sad to being a hellcat. Pounding on his chest with her fists and kicking at him with her feet.

"You asshole. Why did you do that?" Ava's voice broke, the words strangled and shaky.

"To keep them safe. You know it was the right thing to do."

It didn't mean it was the easy thing. It felt like he'd lost a limb as he'd watched that plane disappear into the clouds and sky. But his children wouldn't die in a rain of gunfire.

Sniffling, Ava wiped her face on the hem of her shirt. At some point, the shots had ceased and Jared had run over to what they had thought was a deserted building right next to the tarmac, Griffin right behind him. Reed had stayed to protect Kaylee but now they were all cautiously raising their heads.

Jared waved from the top of the building, his voice booming. "Up here. He was up here."

Was. Did that mean whomever was there was gone now? In the chaos of gunfire and jet engines, Logan hadn't heard or seen a vehicle but he'd been protecting Ava while the others fired back.

And how was Wade in two places at once? He'd been at the safe house kidnapping Amy and now he was here? Logan was triple sure no one had driven up after them so that only left that Wade had known they were coming here and had laid in wait.

That leak in the marshal service was really pissing Logan off. People could have died today. It was just lucky that no one had been hurt.

Probably. Or had Wade just done this to scare him? More games. A man with a sniper rifle that high up and close should have been able to pick them off one by one without much trouble. He wasn't that far away and he'd had the element of surprise. The casualty number should be high.

Cursing under his breath, Logan stood and helped Ava to her feet as Reed did the same to Kaylee. The all still had their weapons drawn but it was eerily quiet now. If Wade had been here, he was gone now.

"We walked right into his trap," Reed said through gritted teeth. "Jesus, I feel stupid. We should have checked the roof of the building."

"We just wanted to get them on the plane," Logan said, his arm still tight around his crying wife. She'd forgive him. Eventually. "We didn't anticipate a sniper."

Kaylee stepped out from behind Reed, both hands pressed against her side. A large crimson stain was growing on her gray t-shirt.

White as a sheet, she reached out a blood-covered hand toward her husband. "Reed, I–"

She would have crumpled to the ground, but Reed caught her before she hit the pavement.

Kaylee had been shot.

CHAPTER TWENTY

Tanner and Seth rushed into the hospital waiting area, breathless and asking a million questions. Reed didn't even budge or turn around from his spot in the hallway right next to a set of double doors. He hadn't moved for over an hour, although Ava had tried to get him to sit down and rest several times.

Kaylee was behind those doors in emergency surgery.

Standing to greet the newcomers, she hugged both men and wiped a stray tear from her cheek. For some reason seeing Tanner and Seth here had the waterworks going again. She'd been trying to be strong for Reed but it wasn't easy. Kaylee was like a sister and if anything happened to her...

Ava couldn't even allow herself to think that way. Kaylee was going to be fine, Reed and Kaylee's marriage was going to be fine, Colt and Brianna were going to be fine, and Logan was going to be fine, although she had no idea where he even was right now. She only knew he and Jared had gone after Wade while she, Griffin, and Reed had rushed Kaylee to the hospital.

Everything was fine. Just dandy. Life was a bowl of cherries. Rainbows and fucking unicorns.

Griffin left his post standing next to Reed to welcome Tanner and Seth to their vigil. They were all supposed to meet at the old airfield and thank goodness they'd been delayed by a traffic accident on the road or they might have been hurt as well.

"How is she?" Tanner asked in a hushed tone, his gaze on Reed although he was speaking to Ava and Griffin. "Have you heard anything?"

Reed was going to hear whatever was said because this hallway was so freakin' quiet Ava could hear a pin drop. For some reason, there was no one bustling around. The lone nurse at the desk had been head down over a stack of files the entire time and hadn't said a single word.

Ava shook her head, the acid from her stomach in the back of her throat. "No, we haven't heard anything. They did say that the surgery could take awhile."

Images of Kaylee in the back of the van, white as a ghost, as Reed had ripped off his jacket and held it over the wound raced back. The blood. There had been so much blood. The men around Ava had been in combat but even they had been affected by what they'd seen. The sheer terror in Reed's expression and the fear in Kaylee's would haunt Ava for the rest of her life.

"If we'd been there—" Seth growled but Ava shook her head and placed her hand on his arm.

"Then you might have been hurt, too."

"Did you get off any shots?" Tanner asked Griffin but he was still looking at Reed, who stood like a marble statue. Waiting. "Did you see Bryson?"

"We got off a few but it wasn't easy to ascertain where the gunfire was coming from. By the time we did, Bryson was pretty much done. Logan thinks that he didn't really want to kill anyone. This was just more of his games."

"Logan has a point," Tanner conceded. "If Bryson wanted

all of you dead, he had a good chance of doing it but he let it go by."

Ava bit her lip and tasted blood. She couldn't say out loud what she was thinking...that Bryson might have actually killed one of them whether he intended to or not. Frankly, she didn't give a fuck what he'd intended. Results were what mattered and if Kaylee—

No, she couldn't think about it because it was making her crazy.

Walking over to Reed, Tanner placed his hand carefully on his friend's shoulder so as not to spook him. "Hey, how about we get you some coffee or maybe a sandwich? You haven't eaten since breakfast, I bet."

Reed simply shook his head slightly, not bothering to verbally answer. His gaze was still trained on those metal double doors.

"She's going to be okay," Tanner finally said when Reed didn't reply or look at him. "Kaylee's a fighter. She always has been. Remember when you first met her and she told you that she didn't need you? She could handle her own stalker? She's a badass and she's going to pull through. You guys got her here really fast and they took her to surgery immediately. She's going to be okay."

Still not moving or speaking, Reed didn't acknowledge his friend. His focus was solely on what lay beyond those doors.

Seth stepped forward, rubbing the back of his neck. "Tanner, why don't you take Ava for coffee and a bite to eat? I'll stay here with Reed and Griffin."

"I don't need—"

"Yes, you do," Tanner interrupted. "It's been hours since you ate. You won't be any good to Kaylee or Logan if you make yourself sick in the process. You have to take care of yourself so that you can take care of them when the time comes. We'll get you a bite to eat and we'll also get coffee for everybody."

She didn't have an argument other than she was afraid that if she left something terrible would happen like Kaylee dying, but she couldn't put that fear into words so she simply nodded and followed Tanner down the hall.

For all of her bravado, Ava was tempted to let Tanner take charge. She was exhausted and she wanted to sleep for a week. Not now though. If she closed her eyes, she'd be tortured with the images of Kaylee fighting for life and it would only make her scream out loud.

Screaming. That's what she wanted to do. Scream as loudly as she possibly could. Would it help?

"Ava."

How long had Tanner been speaking to her? She'd been far away back at the airfield.

"What?"

Tanner looked concerned, his brows pinched together in a frown. "I don't want to be an asshole here, honey, but you look terrible."

She tried to laugh but she couldn't carry it off. It came out choked, half-cough, half-cry for help.

"You're a sweet talker."

"Seriously, you look awful." His fingers brushed her hand. "Ava, did you know you have blood on your hoodie? We can go down to the gift shop and get you another."

Looking down at herself, she realized he was right. She'd been in the back of the van holding Kaylee's hand and some of the blood must have transferred onto her.

So much blood. Everywhere.

"Kaylee was bleeding."

"I know, honey." Tanner grabbed a couple of ready-made sandwiches and an apple along with two sodas. "Let me pay for these and we'll go outside. I saw a few tables. The fresh air will do us good."

After paying, he guided Ava outside to a picnic table in the shade. There wasn't anyone around, the other patrons having chosen to sit inside, and she was glad of the privacy. She didn't need people looking at her wondering what had happened. Heaven forbid a stranger should speak to her. She wasn't equipped for that right now.

He opened her soda can and placed it in front of her along with the apple and sandwich. She wasn't hungry but Tanner was a stubborn cuss. She needed to make it look like she'd eaten or drank something so she took a sip of the sweet beverage, enjoying the cool liquid on her tight throat.

"Have you heard from Evan or Josie yet?" she managed to get out.

"They're still in the air."

With my babies.

But my babies are safe. Safer. But not with me.

They're not with me.

"They're safe as kittens, honey," Tanner said gently, pushing the sandwich closer to Ava. "Try and eat a little for me. We can't have you passing out from hunger. Kaylee's going to need you when she wakes up."

What if she doesn't wake up? It's all my fault. She came here to help me.

Instead of saying all that was running through her head, Ava took a bite of the sandwich. Some sort of grilled chicken. Or turkey. It didn't matter. It mostly tasted like cardboard.

"Seth and I are going to stay here as long as you need us to."

Swallowing another bite, Ava shook her head. "No, you need to go help Logan."

"Until he gets a hold of one of us, we don't know where he

and Jared are."

Which meant Ava didn't know, either. She only knew that he'd gone after Wade. Her husband was a great lawman but even he could make mistakes every now and then. Today was one of those days. They'd let their guard down for only a moment...

Mayhem. Chaos. And maybe death.

Two bites of the sandwich had gone okay but the third simply wasn't going to happen. Gagging on the food in her mouth, Ava stumbled toward the tree, the bark cool and rough under her palm, and let the meager contents of her stomach come back the other way.

At some point as she purged food, drink, acid, and the lining of her stomach and intestines, Tanner had rounded the table and come over to hold her upright. His hand held back her hair as he murmured soft words of encouragement and comfort, none of which she could understand but it was the tone that was the most important. He was speaking to her as if she was about four years old and had found out Santa wasn't real.

Eventually her body had nothing left to give, and her knees collapsed under her. She would have crumpled to the grass, but Tanner simply lifted her up and placed her on the bench again. The smell of the sandwich hit her nostrils and she gagged again until he swept it up and tossed it in a nearby trash can. The soda, however, tasted good and she greedily gulped it even as he cautioned her to slow down, take it easy. She might make herself sick again.

The sticky liquid sloshed down her chin and onto her shirt, and Tanner took it from her trembling hands. Her entire body was shaking, and she had to fold her knees against her chest and wrap her arms around her legs as the sobs really took over.

She'd tried to be strong but it was all too much.

Logan in danger and Kaylee in surgery and her babies on an

airplane. How much was Ava supposed to endure? She'd been married to a man who did dangerous things and she hadn't liked it much. He was supposed to be taking a desk job and staying home all the time.

If he lived long enough to do that.

Tanner patted her shoulder as she rocked back and forth trying to soothe herself at least a little.

"Let it out, Ava. Let it all out. You've been through it and then some. No one would blame you for having a good cry today."

A good cry? She was looking at a *good cry* in the rearview mirror. She was sobbing, and she couldn't seem to stop. The tears went on and on until she was amazed that she had any fluids left in her body after throwing up, too. By the time she was spent her head hurt, her stomach hurt, and every muscle and bone in her body hurt as well.

"I'm scared."

Her words were soft but the plain truth. She was terrified, and no one seemed to understand.

"What are you scared of?"

Her mouth fell open and she stared at Tanner. How could he be this stupid? Was he fucking blind? Or was everyone else in some weird state of denial?

"Because Kaylee could die." She pushed Tanner away and tried to stand up, but the world began to spin and tilt. Unceremoniously, she plopped down on the grass, wiping at her snotty nose and tearstained cheeks. "Because my husband might be walking into a goddamn trap. And because my babies aren't with me. They're not with me, Tanner. How am I supposed to keep them safe when *they're not with me*?"

Her voice had gone up at the end and the last was delivered as an almost scream. She still wanted to do that. Scream until she'd lost her voice. There was no one around. Did she dare give in and just do it?

Coming down onto the ground with her, Tanner pulled a handkerchief out of his pocket and pressed it into her hand. "I know you're upset–"

"Upset," Ava echoed. "That's a weak word for what I feel."

"Okay, I know you're feeling like the world is spiraling out of control–"

"That's a little closer."

"And that everything is dark right now." Ava would have spoken again but Tanner placed his finger over her lips. "Listen to me, because this shit is important. Your husband is one of the best – hell, maybe the best – cop I've seen in my life. Ever, Ava. He knows what the hell he's doing and he knows Bryson. He's going to be fine. We're all going to back him up and I'm not about to let anything happen to him."

"You're here with me."

"As long as you need me to be."

"You should be with him."

"I will be once I'm sure that you're okay."

"I'm okay."

A smile played on his lips and he shook his head. "I'm not so sure about that. Five minutes ago you weren't fine."

She wasn't but she would be.

"I just need some rest and good news."

"You'll get it. Kaylee's going to be fine."

He looked so confident. But he hadn't been there. He hadn't seen what she'd seen.

"You don't know that."

"I know Kaylee and you do, too. Can you imagine a scenario where she just gives up? I can't."

Ava couldn't but...

"You didn't see her. She looked…already gone."

"She'd lost a lot of blood. Doesn't mean she isn't going to make it. I called Maddie about it on the way here. She said that medicine has come a long way with gunshot wounds. Over eighty percent of people shot survive. The odds are good, Ava. Remember Maddie worked in an emergency room, so she's seen the worst of the worst."

That did help a little. It gave Ava hope, although anyone could lie with statistics.

"And your children are safe," Tanner went on. "Evan and Josie are going to take good care of them and they're in the best place they could be. Far away from here."

Logically Ava knew that Colt and Brianna were safe, safer than if they were with her, but emotionally she was a mess.

"But I'm not there. What if they're scared? What if they have a nightmare? Are they going to be scarred for life because they heard gunfire? What are Logan and I doing to our children?"

"Kids are resilient and strong. You'll be talking to them very soon and you'll be able to see that for yourself. Colt and Brianna are lucky to have you and Logan for parents."

She was beginning to think that was bullshit.

"I'm not sure about that. We're terrible parents, dragging them along with us through all of this." Because as much as she wanted to keep her children close, she'd been selfish not sending them away first thing. "What if my babies had been shot?"

Finally. She'd voiced her real fear that had been twisting its way through her gut for hours.

"They weren't. You protected them. You put them on that plane."

"By accident. They wanted to see the inside. They could have been–"

"But they weren't." Tanner leaned closer and tipped her chin up so she had to look at him. His expression was somber, his own eyes bright with tears. "Don't torture yourself with might-have-beens. The reality is serious enough without any of us making it worse by imagining scenarios that could have happened but didn't. You're probably traumatized by what happened so I'm going to give you some advice until you talk to a professional about what you've been through. Live in the moment, Ava. Don't go backward. It will only make this harder. For right now, live in the present."

Tanner was a wise man and it sounded like decent advice. Except that the here and now sucked pretty badly, too.

But she'd try. That's all she could promise. Trying.

CHAPTER TWENTY-ONE

Logan and Jared lay at the top of the hill behind some trees and silently observed the camp below – an ancient, rundown cabin that barely looked able to stand up on its own with a truck parked in front and an old sedan in back. An armed man lounged on a rickety wooden chair by the front door...a door that had only been used once since they'd been watching.

Wade had gone through that door.

As Logan had predicted he'd found Wade, although his childhood friend had made it exponentially easier when he'd made the mistake of ambushing them at the airfield. That move had tipped his hand and Logan had been able to trail them to this location in the mountains. Wade had never been much of an outdoorsman and this camp wasn't the best choice for an on the run serial killer.

It was surrounded on three sides by higher ground and the only way to drive out was one road. It practically begged to be invaded by law enforcement. That might have been why Wade chose it, of course. He had fantasies of a testosterone-filled hail of gunfire, perhaps some hand to hand combat, then he wanted to personally kill Logan. Preferably slow and painful, although he'd do it quick too if he needed to. After all, that's how he'd dispatched the other Bryson males.

Logan wasn't about to let any of that happen. Wade wasn't going to allow himself to go back to prison and he didn't give a shit about innocent lives – as evidenced by the fact that Kaylee was in the hospital fighting for her life at the moment. No, Logan had something far more low-key in mind.

Silently elbowing Jared, Logan pointed over his shoulder. They needed to discuss what they wanted to do now. He had his ideas, but he wasn't averse to listening to his best friends. They climbed over the top of the hill and then down the other side to where the SUV was waiting.

"Do you think Amy and Mike might be alive in that cabin?" Jared asked as they drove away. Logan didn't want them to be caught unawares that close to their camp. They'd take up a position near the lone road in and out but far enough away not to be seen. Eventually, Logan would need to watch the camp closely, taking note of the habits and movements. Only then could he formulate a final plan.

"It's possible," Logan replied, his fingers tapping a beat on the steering wheel. "That's why I think we need to rule out going in with guns blazing. We could do that and we'd win as we have more men, but I don't want innocent people losing their lives if we can avoid that."

At least he thought they outnumbered the bad guys. Wade could have another team somewhere nearby, but Logan's gut was telling him that Wade was a loner. He would only trust a few people. It wasn't in his nature to build an army. He'd create a duo or trio and then get rid of them when they no longer served their purpose. Just like Marilyn. Then he'd go in search of another ally and the cycle would start all over again.

"What are we going to do about the leak?"

Rubbing at his temple, Logan grimaced at the question. "I've been asking myself that since the airfield. Clearly, the marshals have a leak. We just don't know who it is. My feeling is that if we tell the marshals we've found Wade somehow he's going to slip out of the noose and get away. I can't imagine how but I can't trust them. I think until we know who the leak is we need to keep this to ourselves."

"And hope we find Amy and Mike alive."

There was always hope but knowing Wade? The chances weren't in their favor.

Reed didn't know how long he'd been sitting on the hard plastic chair next to Kaylee's hospital bed. Time was all messed up inside this building with its gray walls and antiseptic smell. With the blinds drawn it could have been day or night, summer or winter. He didn't know, and it didn't matter. The only thing that did was lying on that bed unconscious, and it was all his fault.

He'd been greedy, arrogant, and only thinking of himself when Kaylee had told him she was coming along to help Ava with the twins. He'd wanted a chance to spend time with her, try and repair their broken marriage and he'd managed to do that.

But at what cost? The price was far too high.

He should have never let her go and insisted she stay home and be safe even if it meant that they never worked out their issues. Better her to be alive and not with him than the alternative.

He'd made a deal with whatever god might be listening. If Kaylee would only survive, he'd back off. He'd give her whatever space she wanted and if she wanted a divorce then he'd give it to her. When she woke up, she would have every reason to blame him for what had happened and he'd take whatever anger she had because he deserved it. He was the cop. He was supposed to know better.

He didn't hear the door open until Griffin was standing next to him holding out a paper cup of coffee. Steam rose from the contents and the aroma made his empty stomach lurch. The combined smell of coffee, rubbing alcohol, and sickness did nothing for his appetite.

Griffin pulled up another plastic chair and sat down next to Reed. "It's not very good coffee but it might help you stay awake."

Reed didn't need any help. He might never sleep again.

"Thanks." He accepted the cup because it would have been ill-mannered to do anything else. "Did Tanner and Seth leave?"

Griffin nodded. "Just a few minutes ago. Logan didn't want to go into details but they've found the camp. Now they watch and learn the schedule, formulate a plan."

Acid churned in Reed's gut and bile rose in his throat. He'd never hated many people in his life, always thought it was a waste of time and energy, but he hated Wade Bryson with a fire in his belly that he hadn't even known existed in the world. He'd gladly kill the man with his bare hands with a smile on his face the entire time he was doing it. No regrets. Bryson was a blight on humanity and Reed would be doing the world a favor by taking him out of it.

If Kaylee died, there wouldn't be a safe place for Bryson to hide in this universe. Reed would make it his life's mission to—

"Reed," Griffin said loudly. "Are you listening to me?"

No, he hadn't been. He'd been thinking about revenge.

"Sorry, what were you saying?"

"I was saying that Evan, Josie, and the twins made it to Florida. They called and Ava got to talk to Colt and Brianna. Evan is taking them to the beach. He said the kids didn't really see anything. They were elbow deep in chocolate and toys. They did hear the gunfire though which Josie explained away as sounds from the airplane engine. Who really knows if they bought it?"

"They should probably go see a counselor after what happened," Reed replied wryly. "But I guess the ocean is supposed to be healing, too."

"I'm sure Ava and Logan will do that," Griffin said. "They're good parents."

"They are," Reed agreed. "You and Jazz would be good parents."

It was an idle observation, one that Reed had made to keep Griffin from asking tough questions like what the doctor had said.

She was lucky. We repaired the damage and replaced the blood she lost. It's up to Kaylee now. Is your wife a fighter?

That's what the doctor had said.

Kaylee was a fighter, but it was hard to fight and be tough when she was lying in a hospital bed, needles and tubes coming out of her arm and hooked up to monitors. She was as white as the sheet she was lying on, her auburn hair a flame around her pale features. Every now and then she'd sigh or gasp and Reed would come out of his chair, hoping against hope that she'd wake up and every time he'd been disappointed.

It's up to Kaylee now.

Come back to me, honey. I need you.

I can't lose another person I love. Not again.

"We're not going to have any children," Griffin said, taking a sip of his coffee. "I don't mind kids or anything, but I grew up in a full house and it's just not something I want in my adult years."

Griffin was one of about a billion kids in his family and everyone knew that he liked his peace and quiet, but when Jazz had started that theatre group for the kids in the county everyone had just assumed that they would have a couple of children.

Just as everyone had assumed that Reed and Kaylee would have kids.

Staring down at his rapidly cooling coffee, Reed tried to take a drink but his tight throat made it almost impossible to swallow. He ended up coughing and wiping the coffee from his chin.

Griffin slapped at Reed's back. "Easy there. Just sip it, buddy. Take it slow."

"I'm okay. It was just hotter than I expected."

Kaylee hadn't moved despite all the fuss and noise. Her chest rose and fell evenly, her features in peaceful repose.

"Right. So, can I get you something to eat?"

"I'm good."

Apparently that answer wasn't what Griffin wanted to hear. "When was the last time you ate? You should eat something. You won't be any good to anyone if you don't eat."

Reed didn't have enough fingers to count the number of times someone had come into this room and said the exact same thing. He was damn tired of it.

"Stop acting like my mother."

"I'm just trying—"

He'd had enough. There were too many people telling him what to do, what to say, and how to feel. They all thought they knew what he was feeling. They didn't know shit.

"Leave me the fuck alone," Reed said, pushing the chair back so the legs scraped against the gray tile. "I just want to be left alone. Can't you see that?"

"Yes, and that's why we're not doing it."

"Fuck you."

Griffin had almost a dozen siblings and a myriad of cousins

and he wasn't going to be put off by Reed being an asshole.

"Fuck you, too. We're just trying to help you."

"Maybe I don't need help."

"Maybe you need so much help you don't even realize it. You're sitting here swimming in self-pity and that, my friend, isn't doing Kaylee a bit of good so fucking stop it."

Leaping to his feet, Reed got into Griffin's face. Nose to nose. Man to man. It felt good to actually do something, even if it was only feel a little anger.

"Fuck you. Fuck you. *Fuck you!* I'm not swimming in self-pity but if I was, wouldn't it be justified? I might lose another wife. That would be two while you're still on number one, you son of a bitch."

"And that's not fair," Griffin agreed. "Not fair at all and I cannot imagine what hell you're going through."

"Then why are you acting this way?"

"Because I'm thinking about Kaylee. You're thinking about you."

The intimation that Reed wasn't thinking about the woman he loved before himself was just the match to the fuse that he needed to go off. Before he could stop himself, he'd punched Griffin right on the jaw, sending him staggering back a few steps.

"Do you feel better now?" Griffin laughed, wiping a trickle of blood from the corner of his mouth with the back of his hand. "I'd hit you back, but this is a goddamn hospital and your wife is lying there fighting for her life. A little fact you seemed to forget for a moment. I'll put that punch in the bank though so when you least expect it, expect it, asshole."

His face hot, Reed sat back down heavily in the chair. He had forgotten where he was for a moment and he wasn't proud of that. And now his hand hurt.

"I don't feel better," he admitted, rubbing at the reddened knuckles. "I'm sorry."

"I know you are, but you still owe me a free shot. Listen to me because I'm getting tired of trying to help your ungrateful ass. You're awash in guilt and self-pity and that's not going to help Kaylee. It's indulgent and selfish to do this. It doesn't help her or you, by the way, it only serves to put distance between the two of you. It's not your fault Kaylee was shot. There. I said it out loud."

"How did you know—"

"It's written all over your face, and also Tanner made a few remarks before he left. We can all see it and I can assure that it's not a productive emotion. Guilt fools you. It makes you think you're doing a whole bunch, but in reality you're just swimming laps in a riptide and getting pulled under. Next thing you know you have to fight to get to the surface or be drowned by it."

It was almost exactly what Reed and Ava had said to Kaylee this week. It appeared he'd come full circle. Now he was the one wracked with guilt. Griffin was right. It would only put a barrier between Reed and Kaylee when they'd just knocked the last one down.

"If I'd said no when she wanted to come—"

"She would have come anyway," Griffin finished for him. "Let's face it. We're not exactly married to shrinking violets. Our women kick ass. They're stubborn and brave and fiercely loyal. Kaylee would have come to help Ava because that's what friends do. I'm here, aren't I? I could be fishing, you know."

No one loved their quiet fishing trips more than Griffin.

"I just want her to be okay."

"She will be. She's tough and she loves you. The important thing," Griffin went on, "is not to let shit like that fester inside of you. Let it out. If something is bothering you, talk about it.

Express your feelings."

"That sounds horrifying."

"I know it does, doesn't it? But being with Jazz has changed me. She's all about getting in touch with our feelings and talking through them. Being introspective and getting to the root of issues. At first, I thought it was kind of stupid but she's on to something here, man. This shit works and I'd be the first to tell you that I thought it was New Age touchy-feely crap."

"It is New Age touchy-feely crap."

"Well, women like it. You going to be a Neanderthal your whole life?"

"Maybe." He paused before going on. "I can't lose her, Griffin. If I do… Fuck, I can't even imagine it."

Actually, he could and it wasn't pretty. He'd lost Julie and it had taken him years to recover. He didn't think he'd come back from it a second time.

"Good. Keep your thoughts positive. That's what Jazz would say. She'd send all that positivity into the universe."

Reed wanted to believe. If he lost Kaylee, it would be like a hand reaching into his chest and ripping out his heart.

Come back to me, honey. I love you so much.

CHAPTER TWENTY-TWO

Logan stowed his phone back in his pocket. "Kaylee is still not awake so Griffin is going to stay at the hospital to watch over everyone. I tried to convince Ava to go to a hotel to get some rest, but she told me to go fuck myself. So I'm going to take that as a *no*."

Seth snickered and tried to cover it with a cough. "Maybe she'll get some rest once Kaylee wakes up."

"Doctors are really happy about her vital signs," Logan replied. Kaylee was a strong woman. She had a long recovery ahead of her, but Reed would be there every step of the way. "Good and strong. She should wake up soon. In the meantime, it's just us. Reed and Griffin are staying there."

Even without Reed and Griffin, there were enough of them to take down Wade Bryson. The group lounging around a campfire included Tanner, Seth, Jason, and Jared.

And no one had called the marshal service. The other marshals had fanned out over three states to find Wade and they currently had no idea that he'd been found.

That was an issue. The leak could be anywhere, it didn't have to be in the field. Someone pushing paper in a windowless office could be selling them out.

"Are we going to call the marshals?" Tanner asked. "I'm not pushing to do it, I just think we need to decide once and for all."

"I'm against it," Seth piped up. "Too risky."

Jason and Jared were both nodding in agreement.

"I agree," Logan replied. "It's way too risky. If we tell the marshals where Wade is we could be walking into a trap. And Ava has specifically forbidden me to walk into a trap," Logan said with a grin, although he wasn't feeling particularly jolly. "Your wives have as well so we're not going to do that."

"So we do this alone," Tanner said, his expression somber. "And as a team. Now let's get down to business. We need to finalize a plan."

"We go in right before dawn," Logan began. He'd been thinking about this since they'd found the camp. Hell, he'd been thinking about it since he'd heard that Wade had escaped. "From what we've seen Wade only has two men with him. First task is to take out his protection."

Second? I'm sending Wade back to prison. Or a body bag. His choice.

Reed hated the hospital so fucking much. He'd spent far too many hours, days, and weeks in them in his youth and few of those memories were good. Images of Julia lying in a hospital bed had come back to haunt him. Just like then, he was powerless to do anything. He could only sit on this hard plastic chair and wait. Just wait. And hope and pray too, but he'd done that before and it hadn't helped.

The doctor had come in about an hour ago and had given Reed good news. Kaylee was strong, her vital signs excellent, and it would be only a matter of time before she woke up. She'd have a long hard road ahead of her but it looked like she would recover. He had to keep saying that over and over in his head so he could finally believe it.

Kaylee would live.

"Reed…"

His name came out hoarse and rusty. Her throat had to feel like sandpaper after her surgery this morning. Immediately he was at her side, holding her hand and offering her some water from a straw.

She's okay. She's awake.

"Can you hear me, baby?"

She nodded and blinked a few times, still heavily medicated. Her eyes were glassy and voice was still thin and wispy as she took a sip from the straw. "Yes…I can hear you."

He leaned closer so she could easily hear him and ran his fingers across her cheek. So soft. He'd never felt anything as soft as Kaylee's skin or as silky as her auburn hair.

"Baby, do you know where you are?"

She took another drink and then nodded.

"Hospital."

The doctor had warned Reed not to expect too much the first time she woke up. He said she'd be confused and possibly agitated but to simply be calm. Temporary memory loss was common in these situations. Honestly, Reed wouldn't blame her if she didn't want to remember.

"Yes, you were brought here after we were ambushed at the airfield. Do you remember that?"

She frowned and shook her head and he lightly placed his hand on her shoulder, well above her bandages. "That's okay. You don't have to remember anything right now. You just have to rest and get better."

She seemed to relax and accepted another sip of water. The reality was beginning to hit him across the face.

Kaylee was alive, and she was going to stay that way.

"You're going to be okay," Reed assured her, tears beginning to fall down his cheeks, carving a path through his unshaven face. His heart felt too big for his chest. He loved this woman more than anything in the world. "They did surgery and they took out your spleen. You lost a hell of a lot of blood but the doctor says you're lucky. We're lucky, baby. God, I love you so fucking much. You're my world, Kaylee. If anything had happened to you, I wouldn't want to go on. I love you. I love you."

She didn't get a chance to reply. The door to the room swung open and a smiling older nurse bustled in. "Are we awake? That's wonderful. I've alerted the doctor. Mr. Mitchell, I'm going to have to ask you to step out for a little while so we can check her over."

The nurse – Helen, perhaps – was messing with the IV bag and was far too happy for the current circumstances.

"What do you need to do?"

"Just check her over." The nurse patted Kaylee's arm. "It's good that she's awake but she needs her sleep. The doctor will give her something so she rests tonight. She can have more visitors in the morning."

"But I can come back in?"

"In just a few minutes," the nurse assured him. "Go have a bite to eat."

Food was completely out of the question. It would come straight back up. But a call to Logan might be good.

Leaning down, he brushed his lips over Kaylee's. "I'll be right back, baby. I love you."

"Love." Kaylee yawned widely, her eyelids fluttering. She was already beginning to fall back asleep. "You."

"Wore herself out, poor thing," the nurse said. "She'll sleep mostly for the next twenty-four hours or so, only waking for a few minutes here and there. She's heavily medicated. Don't be surprised if later she doesn't remember any of her first few days in the hospital. It's probably better, if I'm honest."

"You think so?"

"I do. Now don't you worry about this young lady. She's in good hands here. Go have a bite to eat or get some sleep. She's really going to need you in a few days when she starts to be awake more."

He'd be there for her. No matter what. There wasn't anything Reed wouldn't do for Kaylee.

Anything.

"She'll sleep all night?"

"Like a baby. This would be a good time for you to catch some rest too, if you can. There's a nice little motel a few blocks away. We can call you if anything changes."

He didn't need rest.

But there was one thing that he needed to do.

Get Wade Bryson and make him pay for what he'd done to Kaylee. Logan had said that Bryson would be behind bars by breakfast.

That wasn't soon enough.

Ava accepted the steaming cup of coffee from Griffin and took a sip. It was late and the hospital was quiet as visiting hours were over.

"Thank you," she said, eyeing the extra cup that he'd set on the coffee table in the waiting area. "Where's Reed?"

Frowning, Griffin looked around the room. "He's in with Kaylee...right?"

Ava shook her head, her mind racing to several conclusions

and hopefully all of them were wrong. "I thought he was with you. He came out of Kaylee's room about an hour ago. He said they were going to give her something to sleep all night. I assumed he was going to find a couch to sack out on or maybe get a bite to eat."

Swearing under his breath, Griffin pulled his phone from his pocket. "I never saw him downstairs. I bet I know where he is, though."

It didn't take a genius to figure out that Reed had taken the opportunity while Kaylee slept to go find Wade. He'd probably kill him too, with his bare hands. Assuming he got there before Logan did, of course.

"I'll let Logan know. I can't say that I blame him. I would do the same if it were Jazz."

Ava had no doubt that all the men would go after anyone that hurt their wives.

"We should have anticipated this."

Griffin paused and looked up from his phone. "Would you have stopped him?"

An interesting question. Part of her thought he should be here even though Kaylee would be sleeping all night and wouldn't know the difference. The other part of her was cheering him on.

"No," she finally replied. "I wouldn't have. I just wish he would have told us when he left."

"He probably thought we'd try and talk him out of it."

That's when it hit her that there was one remaining person on the team who wasn't going to be there when they brought Wade Bryson in. Griffin.

"You can go if you want," she assured him. "We'll be fine here. They aren't going to try anything in a hospital and Logan has Wade under surveillance anyway."

Griffin grinned and took a drink of his coffee. "My job is to protect you and Kaylee. I don't need to be in on the action. It's not personal to me like it is to Logan or Reed. I'm happy to do my part and my part is to take care of you while Logan goes and does what he needs to do. Hopefully this will all be over in the morning."

All over. Wade back behind bars and Ava reunited with Colt and Brianna. She made a mental note to apologize to them for being a lousy parent. All the men could go back to their wives and Kaylee…

Kaylee would have months of painful recovery in front of her. For her, it wouldn't be over in the morning. It would only be just starting.

Because of me.

Ava had mentally scarred her children and physically scarred her best friend. She'd been arrogant and selfish thinking that Wade Bryson couldn't really touch them. That somehow they'd all get through this unscathed while the body count piled up around them.

But now Wade had hit close to home, drawing blood on one of their own. He'd brought all of this on himself.

Logan and Reed weren't going to fail when the time came. An end had come to Wade Bryson's reign of terror.

CHAPTER TWENTY-THREE

The others were asleep and would be for another hour or so. They'd all agreed that they needed to get some rest before going in right before dawn to take down Wade and his little gang. Logan had volunteered to keep watch. He knew he wouldn't sleep anyway.

But Logan had always known what was really going to happen. No one else was going to get hurt or die on his watch.

This was between him and Wade.

And it would be settled between them.

No one knew the importance of working as a team more than Logan. He'd been in the military after all, but this was the exception. After what had happened to Kaylee he wasn't taking any more chances. He'd take Wade one on one. They'd started this whole clusterfuck of a situation years ago and they'd end it.

Slipping silently down the hill, Logan hid behind some pine trees that overlooked the front door of the cabin. He and his friends had been watching the camp for hours and had come to the conclusion that there were only three people there. Wade and two other men. There was no sign of any hostages, unfortunately. The chances of finding Amy and Mike alive were low.

Crickets chirped, and the wind rustled the leaves but all else was quiet and dark, save for one lone man sitting outside the door of the cabin. He had to take him out first without alerting the other inhabitants. There was a wide expanse of clearing that he needed to cross without being seen and the night sky was cloudy playing peekaboo with the bright light of the full moon. That was going to make this operation more difficult. He'd never know from one minute to the next whether he'd be bathed in moonlight or shrouded in darkness.

If they'd gone in as a team, it would all be pretty straightforward. A team member would toss a smoke grenade into the cabin while the others took care of the guard outside. If Wade and the other guy didn't come out, they'd go in and get him. Either way, the numbers were on Logan's side and the entire operation would be done in minutes.

But they weren't going in as a team.

The lilting whistle of a bird in the trees captured Logan's attention. No bird would be singing at night like that which only meant one thing...

Reed.

Logan watched as his friend of many years appeared out of the shadows, his footsteps silent. Reed wasn't supposed to be here. No one was.

"Fuck," Logan hissed quietly. "What in the hell are you doing here?"

"Same thing you are."

"You're supposed to be with your wife."

"The nurse said she's going to sleep all night. By morning we'll either be heroes or dead, I'm thinking."

"You can't be here."

Reed quirked an eyebrow. "Because it's personal for you? Fuck that shit. It's personal for me now, too."

"It's more personal for me."

"We are not going to have this conversation. We both have good reasons for standing here. Now just admit that you need help and let's get this done. The sun will be up soon."

"I don't need your help."

"You're getting it, so shut the hell up and let's get a fucking plan." Reed nodded toward the sleepy guard slouching in his chair. "I figure he's first."

The sun would be up soon and that would necessitate an entirely different approach. Logan didn't have time to argue with his friend and besides, Reed made a decent case. There was no question that Logan would go after anyone who dared harm a hair on top of Ava's head. Reed wanted revenge and Logan wanted Wade out of his life. They both had the same goal so they might as well work together.

"Okay, but I'm in charge."

It was too dark to actually see but Logan was sure he could *hear* Reed roll his eyes.

"Whatever, let's do this. I need to get back to the hospital."

"Does Ava and Griffin know you're here?"

"By now they probably do."

Logan had turned off his phone and left it back at camp. He'd have dozens of messages when he turned it back on later.

"I'm getting too old for this shit," Logan muttered, crouching down farther behind the trees. Reed did the same. "It was easier when I was single."

"Everything's easier when you're young and dumb. We didn't know enough to be scared. We have a hell of a lot more to live for now."

That was true. Logan didn't fancy dying here on this hill. He wanted to grow old with Ava. Step one? Get rid of the biggest interference in their lives. Wade Bryson.

"Listen closely," Logan whispered, his gaze on the guard. "Here's the plan."

✧ ✧ ✧ ✧

Reed's job was to take out the guard in front of the cabin while Logan went around back and threw a smoke grenade into one of the windows. It would hopefully force the two inhabitants out into the open.

That was the plan, anyway.

As soon as a gray cloud passed over the luminous moon, Reed sprinted silently across the clearing and took up a position behind a stack of firewood before counting to one hundred. He could clearly see the guard, who was lousy at his job because his firearm was sitting on the ground next to him instead of in his hands. As predicted, waiting to go in had made the fugitives lax and a little lazy. They'd assumed that Logan would come in guns blazing hours ago and when that didn't happen, they'd let their guard down slightly.

That's all Reed and Logan needed.

Ninety-eight, ninety-nine, one hundred.

It happened fast and as quiet as Reed could manage. The guard jerked and grabbed Reed's arms, trying to dislodge his grip. When that failed, he lowered one hand and grunted as he delivered a blow to Reed's midsection with his elbow. Reed nearly doubled over, but he never let up on his grip. This was for Kaylee. The man stomped on Reed's instep, forcing Reed to swing the man around and smash his face against the ground. Using what was left of his strength, he increased the pressure until the guard's eyes fluttered closed and his body went limp.

The guard might be crumpled on the ground, but as soon as the blood started to flow again this guy was going to wake up in a minute and be incredibly pissed off. And cranky.

After slapping cuffs on the guard's wrists, Reed shoved a rag in his mouth and then tied a gag around it. He didn't need much time to find Wade, only a few minutes, and that's what this would buy them. Neither Reed nor Logan were looking to kill a man they'd never met and didn't know from Adam. Let the justice system sort them out.

Dragging him around the side of the cabin, Reed placed the guard, who was already beginning rouse, several feet from the structure where he would be out of the way.

Logan had worked his way from the back of the cabin to the doorway on the porch and was signaling with his arm.

The sound of breaking glass indicated Logan had tossed the smoke grenade into the cabin. Not wanting to be in the way when the inhabitants came out, Reed dashed to the security of the vehicle and hid behind it. Logan went somewhere, disappearing into the darkness. A few seconds later, the door flung open and two men stumbled out, coughing and firing into the darkness. They sprinted across the clearing toward the tree-covered hill.

Ducking down as a few flying bullets bounced off the vehicle, Reed crawled near the back bumper and shot at the fleeing figure. Footsteps sounded to Reed's right and he caught sight of Logan in hot pursuit of someone headed in the opposite direction, giving Reed an open field to bring down the other guy.

This one's for Kaylee.

He wasn't as young as he used to be, but if he couldn't chase down a bad guy then he ought to hang up his badge. Leaving the relative safety of the truck as a shield, Reed sprinted across the clearing behind the fleeing man, his lungs aching from sucking in the chilled night air. The guy stopped at one point and haphazardly shot a few times into the darkness, the muzzle flash giving away his location, before setting off again toward the hill.

No one said criminals were brain trusts.

The other guy was getting tired too, because Reed was now easily gaining on him. Pretending he wasn't over forty, he lunged and dropped the man to the ground with a thump that knocked the air out of both of them and sent the fugitive's firearm sliding a few feet away. Surprisingly, there was still fight in the guy as he kicked himself free with enough force to be able to throw a punch. It sent Reed sprawling into the dirt, gasping for air. The man stretched out his arm for the dropped gun. Not in a position to kick the firearm away, Reed only had one option.

It all played out in a split second but the result was the fugitive lying in a pool of his own blood while Reed fell back onto his knees, his breathing ragged and steam coming out of his mouth as he gulped in oxygen. The thud of footsteps in his ears had him whirling around but a figure was there holding up his hands and yelling.

"Don't shoot. I'm Marshal Mike Dayton with the US Marshal Service. Don't shoot."

Jesus, Mary, and the camel. Mike was still alive? Miracles do occur every now and then. Reed pushed himself to his feet and wiped the blood trickling from his mouth with his sleeve.

"We thought you were dead."

It may not have been the most elegant thing to say but it was the truth. Last Reed had heard, they'd only seen three men at the cabin and none of them had been Mike Dayton.

Chuckling, Mike lowered his hands and leaned down to inspect the body. "There were several times I thought I was, too. They took me hostage and kept me tied to a chair. I was able to get out of the ropes but hadn't managed to make a break for it until your very convenient smoke grenade. Who else is here?"

"Logan." Reed nodded toward the east. "He's gone after Bryson."

"Good. That's good. We need to call 911 and let them know we're out here. They can send in reinforcements."

The clouds had finally passed by and the harsh moonlight shone down on the clearing again, giving Reed an excellent view of the marshal. For a hostage, Mike looked pretty damn healthy. Relaxed too, although that could be explained by being rescued. Reed's gaze wandered down to the marshal's wrists.

Not one mark. If he'd been tied up and wriggled out of ropes, then Reed was a monkey's uncle. Marshall Mike Dayton was the leak.

Adrenaline rushing through his veins, Reed lifted his gun just as Mike straightened up, holding the dead man's firearm. It was a standoff and only one of them was going to win.

"The obvious question. Why?" Reed asked.

Smirking, Mike lifted the gun higher so it was pointing directly at Reed's chest. "For the excitement. Do you know how fucking boring my job is?"

Anger churned in Reed's gut and he didn't bother to hold in the snarl that escaped his lips. This asshole was looking for shits and giggles while the body count piled up?

While the woman Reed loved was lying in a goddamn hospital?

"For the excitement," Reed parroted, hardly believing his ears. "That's some sick shit. People died."

Mike shrugged. "People die every day. They probably lived useless lives anyway, going to work every morning and doing some stupid job. Then they go home at night and eat dinner and watch TV, maybe fuck their wife if they're lucky. But probably not because they're losers. They're numb. Completely numb. But not me. I'm wide awake."

"This is being wide awake? Following a narcissistic sociopath on a killing spree?"

Mike smiled and held out his arms wide. "What can I say? I'm living my best life."

"How did you even get with Wade? You didn't work at the prison and you were never on any of his transfer details."

"That's true." Mike chuckled, clearly enamored by the story. "It's funny how life works out. I was bored and looking for excitement when I was contacted by a guy who had been in Wade's cell block. I was in a mentoring program for the guy's son while he was in prison."

"Sounds like you were a lousy mentor."

"It's the luckiest thing I've ever done. I've never felt more alive than when I was on that roof shooting down at all of you, watching you scurry like rats in a gutter."

Mike had been the one that shot Kaylee. Not Wade. Anger and fury rushed through Reed's veins with a white-hot heat that almost brought him to his knees. He wanted to rip Mike into tiny pieces with his bare hands. He wanted to make the crooked marshal suffer and pay for his crimes. The justice system didn't have a punishment fit for what Mike had done to Kaylee.

It was only a split second but that's all that Reed needed. For a mere moment Mike was distracted with his celebration, reliving his glories as one of Wade's henchmen and Reed didn't hesitate. With a roar of pure unadulterated rage Reed tackled the younger man to the ground, knocking the air out of both of them but he didn't care. The blood rushed in his ears as his world narrowed to the here and now and his vision filled with red, never giving the dirty lawman a chance. Straddling the marshal and pinning him down, Reed landed one punch after another, hearing the cracking of Mike's nose and feeling the warm spurt of crimson on his hand and sleeve.

He still didn't stop, his fists next going after the marshal's soft gut until all the fight leaked from his adversary and he lay limp on the ground. Mike would live to face the real justice system, of course, but he'd be doing it with a broken nose and a couple of cracked ribs. Retrieving Mike's gun from where it had been dropped, Reed then reached for the satellite phone to call Tanner and the others.

"That was for Kaylee."

Now he needed to go find Logan and Wade.

CHAPTER TWENTY-FOUR

W ade might have been an overweight out of shape businessman at one point but that was years ago. He'd slimmed down in prison and in addition to becoming more cold, calculated, and dangerous, had obviously started working out.

Perhaps in preparation for this moment. Knowing Wade as he did, Logan hadn't been all that shocked when his so-called brother had broken out of prison. He was never going to live the rest of his life there and he sure as hell didn't intend to go back.

Sprinting after Wade in the dark, Logan grunted with the effort as branches smacked at his arms, legs, and head. He'd be scratched and bruised when the sun came up in a little while. Or he'd be dead. That was a possibility, although Logan had – as Reed had said earlier – a hell of a lot to live for. What did Wade have? Nothing. No one loved him and he didn't give a shit about anyone but himself. That was no way to live.

That gave Logan the advantage. His will to survive. He wouldn't give up but Wade wasn't a man that liked struggle. Even his kills had been relatively easy with victims that wouldn't put up much of a fight. Wade liked the simple targets and Logan wasn't one of them.

Stopping abruptly in a small clearing circled by pine trees, Wade turned around to face Logan. The son of a bitch pointed his gun at Logan. And smiled. Because this was all a fucking game to the bastard.

So Logan would play. For a little while. Just to see what Wade had planned.

There the two of them stood about twenty feet apart, moonlight glinting off the barrels of their guns pointed at one another. The clouds had cleared and it was as bright as day. Logan could clearly see Wade's jubilant expression. The son of a bitch was happy.

Wade cackled, his grin spreading across his face. "I knew it would be you."

I'll just humor him.

"Of course, you did."

They were both breathing heavily, puffs of steam appearing when they spoke. Wade wasn't wearing a coat, only a flannel button down over a t-shirt and a pair of jeans. He'd either been sleeping in his boots or he'd stopped to put them on when the smoke grenade went off.

"I did. I knew it would be you coming after me. You know this is between us. We've both always known that even when we were kids."

Logan doubted that as a child he'd known that he'd be standing here pointing a gun at one of his friends and he also doubted that Wade knew that.

"We were friends back then. Not enemies."

"We're not enemies now. We're brothers, Logan. We're more alike than different."

More of this bullshit.

"That seems to be a subject you're stuck on, Wade. You want us to be the same but we're not. I'm not a cold-blooded killer."

"Then you're not going to shoot me? How disappointing. I was sure you would. You're a Bryson, after all."

"I'm not a Bryson. You're a Bryson. Who killed his own brothers. Why, Wade?"

"They were evil just like Dad was. It's in the Bryson blood, brother. You can't escape it."

Wade had become slightly nuttier in the last few days on the run.

"How were they evil? They didn't kill anyone. You did that."

Wade shrugged. "They might as well have. They lied, cheated, and stole. They were only a fraction of the way from taking a life. I just stopped them before they did."

"No one is completely innocent, but I don't think Lyle would have ever killed someone. He was your little brother, man, and you shot him in the head. That's some cold shit. Lyle loved you."

Keep him talking. Get into his psyche.

"He hated me for what I did to the Bryson family name." Wade laughed again. "Can you imagine that? The Bryson family name. As if that's anything to be proud of. Dad and Uncle George made sure that we would always be keeping our head down, didn't they?"

"It's one thing to be dishonest in business but that's not equal to taking a life, Wade. What you've done is evil. What they did was bad. But there's no moral equivalence there. One is far worse than the other. You've killed innocent people for fun. Because you enjoy it. You're not killing criminals anymore that slipped through the justice system. You're doing it because it excites you. Isn't that right?"

Wade didn't argue, instead nodding in agreement. "Yes, the Bryson blood is evil. That's why you're here, Logan. To kill me."

"I'm not here to kill you. I'm here to take you in. You're going back to prison."

"I don't think so. Next stop for me is Florence. I won't go. You'll have to kill me or I'll kill you. You're more like me than you know, my brother. Everyone thinks that you're a hero but you like killing just as much as I do. You only pretend that you don't. You've wrapped up your murder in righteousness but you and I know the truth, don't we? You like it. I like it."

Logan wasn't going to argue with Wade about whether he enjoyed killing. He didn't but his half-brother would never believe it. Even now Logan didn't want to kill Wade, but he would if he had to.

"What would killing me accomplish? You'd still be alive. The Bryson evil would still be in the world."

Was this some sort of murder-suicide thing? Was that what Wade had in mind?

"Did you ever hear that story about the scorpion and the frog? The scorpion asks the frog for a ride across the pond and the frog of course says no. He's afraid of getting stung. But the scorpion assures the frog that he won't do that. If he did then they would both drown and that doesn't make any sense. So the frog gives the scorpion a ride and halfway across the pond, he feels a sting on his back. He asks the scorpion why he did it because now they're both going to drown. The scorpion says, 'It's in my nature to sting'."

"It's in your nature to sting," Logan repeated, his arm getting tired. Wade's had to be getting tired, too. "That's the stupidest story I've ever heard in my fucking life. Where did you hear that?"

"Marilyn told me in one of my therapy sessions. I miss her sometimes."

"You killed her when she wasn't any use to you anymore.

Which reminds me, is Marshal Amy Sinclair alive?"

"Sadly no, but she put up more of a fight than the other ones."

Jesus, Logan would never get used to the death and destruction this one man wreaked upon the planet. How on earth could they share the same blood and DNA?

Snapping his teeth together, Logan's jaw hurt where he gritted them together. "Where is her body, Wade? We have to notify her next of kin."

"I don't remember exactly. Somewhere near your safe house. Strange name...safe house. You were never safe there. I always knew where you were."

Now they were getting somewhere.

"We assumed you had someone inside the marshal service."

"I certainly did. Mike has been invaluable letting me know all of your movements."

Mike Dayton? Wade spoke of him as if he was still alive. Where in the hell was he?

Can't worry about that. Focus on Wade. Reed will deal with the others.

"Mike can't help you now. It's just you and me."

"That's right, it is." Wade held up his gun, waving it around. "And this is a horrible way to go out of the world. It needs to be you and me. Brother against brother. Fists against fists. What do you say? On three, we both toss these guns aside and duke it out like we used to when we were kids. What did we used to say? Fair and square. Winner take all, Logan."

Wade might have been honing his badass routine in prison for the last few years, but Logan hadn't exactly gone soft during the same time period.

"We both know who would win. I'm a decorated war hero who has been trained to kill in hand to hand combat in the Army Rangers. You're some guy that acts tough around the prison yard. The odds are definitely not in your favor, Wade."

"I don't think they're as bad as you say. Maybe you're afraid?"

Logan snorted. "Next you're going to double dog dare me. We're not ten anymore."

Wade's smile widened on his face. At that moment he looked more like that man that Logan had known all those years ago, boyish and innocent. "No, we're not. We're grown men. Brothers. You're just like me, Logan. You're a Bryson."

"The last fucking thing I am is a Bryson."

Logan's declaration was like a starter's pistol at the beginning of a race. It set Wade off roaring like a bear. His gun pointed straight at Logan's chest, he barreled toward him screaming like a banshee. No actual words. Just a war cry that could be heard for miles.

With reflexes that had been honed in battle, Logan didn't hesitate. He pulled the trigger twice, hitting Wade both times. One in the head and one in the heart.

Wade Bryson, vigilante serial killer, seemed to waver on his feet after the first bullet but his legs gave out when hit the second time. His expression wasn't one of shock or surprise but happiness.

Happy that Logan had shot and killed him.

In his mind, that makes us the same. We're not. The difference between Wade and me? I didn't want to do it and he did.

Wade didn't want to go back to prison so he'd made what looked like the ultimate sacrifice. Himself. Logan knew it was bullshit. This was all to prove a point.

Wade had failed spectacularly. There were too many ways to count in which they were different. He never did understand it because he wasn't capable.

So many deaths, so many lives ripped apart because Wade

had so many things to prove. In the end, he only proved that he didn't care about anyone but himself. Now he couldn't hurt anyone anymore.

Sucking oxygen into his starved lungs, Logan stared down at Wade's prone body. In the end, Wade had received what he'd wanted. He'd gone out in blaze of gunfire. This would make the papers and then, God willing, Wade and his reign of terror would be forgotten.

"I called Tanner. The team will be here soon. Cops too, I would imagine."

Reed.

Logan turned to see his friend, looking alive and well.

"How long were you standing there?"

"Long enough."

"You had every reason to kill him and you had the shot."

"I did," Reed agreed as the sound of a chopper filled the air. The cavalry was here. "But you had things in hand. Mike was the leak, by the way. He'll definitely live to make a statement."

Logan felt tired. Exhausted. He wanted to curl up with Ava and sleep for days. He wanted to kiss her and hold her and tell her he loved her. He wanted to hold Colt and Brianna and then watch them grow up. He wanted to hold Ava's hand for the rest of his life.

"I could use a beer. How about it?"

Reed chuckled and rubbed his jaw. "Naw, I think I'll head back to the hospital. Kaylee's going to need me. As it is I'm going to have to explain this bruise."

And Ava would need Logan. That's how he was different than Wade. He was loved and he loved in return. There was nothing better.

CHAPTER TWENTY-FIVE

Kaylee leaned heavily on Reed's arm as he helped her into the front door of Ava and Logan's home in a quiet suburb outside of Seattle. The location was ideal for her long recovery – close to hospitals and doctors but not smack dab in the middle of the bustling city.

Ava hovered nearby, her arms outstretched in case Kaylee decided to do a somersault or something crazy like that. "We can set you up in the guest bedroom or in the living room on the recliner. Are you thirsty? I can get you some food. Or hungry? I can fix something."

Colt and Brianna were looking at their mother as if she'd lost her marbles babbling that way. Kaylee, for her part, thought that her friend was being very sweet if a tad too overwrought.

"I think I'd like to sit in the living room if you don't mind. I've been lying down far too much these last few weeks."

Although the hospital hadn't coddled Kaylee for long. As soon as they could, they'd had her up and walking the halls of the hospital even when she still had her IV in. She hadn't been too happy about it, either. It had taken so much effort to take even a few steps that she'd be exhausted and hurting for a long time afterward. Her new reality was that every little action took effort and would for awhile longer. The doctors said she was healing quickly but it was still going to take some time before she was one hundred percent.

Her husband's strong arms helped lower her slowly into the soft leather chair. A sheen of sweat had popped out on her upper lip and the back of her neck and her abdomen was sore. It had been a long drive from the rural hospital she'd been in originally to Seattle. Reed had made her as comfortable as he could, but she hurt and needed a couple of ibuprofen. The pillow that had become a much-needed accessory was placed on her stomach. She used it when she needed to cough, sneeze, or even just turn over in bed. Reed had dubbed it her teddy bear. Today she'd used it as a buffer between herself and the seatbelt.

Hovering. Everyone hovered around her as she was going to explode into a million little pieces at any moment.

Heck, maybe I will and the doctors just didn't warn me.

Dropping a kiss on her forehead before straightening, Reed turned to help Logan with the luggage.

"Do you need anything?" Ava asked again, anxiety in her voice. "Anything at all?"

"Just to sit and relax a bit. Why don't you sit down, too?"

"Easy, baby," Reed said, reaching down for the lever on the side of the recliner. "I'm going to help you stretch out a little, okay?"

Kaylee nodded gratefully and almost sighed audibly in relief as her legs were lifted and her torso angled back. Being folded up was the worst thing for her surgery incision but every day she was getting better. It hadn't hurt that this handsome son of a gun had been there by her side twenty-four-seven. He'd been her rock and she'd clung to him. Funny how now she could hardly believe that she'd doubted his love or commitment. He'd shown it in so many ways these last few weeks.

The living room and kitchen were one big room and the island was covered with flowers and plants, balloons, and actual teddy bears, not just soft pillows. Ava followed Kaylee's gaze and smiled.

"Those are all for you. The pink roses are from Griffin and Jazz, the potted plant with the teddy bear is from Tanner and Madison, the bright purple flower arrangement is from Dare and Rayne, the flower basket is from Seth and Presley, the chocolates are from Evan and Josie, the stack of DVDs are from Jared and Misty, and the refrigerator is stacked with food courtesy of Jason and Brinley. They had a restaurant deliver all sorts of amazing-looking dishes so if you're hungry you only have to say something and we can warm it up."

Kaylee's throat had tightened with emotion and tears pricked the backs of her eyes. "I'm...overwhelmed."

"We love you," Ava said softly, her own eyes looking bright. "And Colt and Brianna have something for you, too."

The twins were still looking at their mother oddly. They probably didn't get all the emotion that was zipping around the room. They'd been safely ensconced in Florida having a great time at the beach and then later with their parents at Disney. To them this had been a grand adventure they could tell their friends about.

Brianna was the first to approach Kaylee. "We drew you pictures. This is you at the beach. Colt drew you with Mickey ears."

Colt scowled at his sister. "I was gonna tell her that."

Brianna pointed to Colt's drawing. "She can see it. You made the ears bigger than her head."

Indeed, the hat was at least twice the size of Kaylee's head and took up most of the paper.

"I think these are wonderful." Her words came out choked. Her heart was so full today. Full of love and gratitude. "Thank you so much. I'm going to hang these by my bed. They'll help me get better faster."

"When you get better you can go to the beach. It was so much fun. We made sandcastles with Josie," Brianna said. "Colt found a hermit crab in the sand."

Colt nodded. "Josie said we had to leave it there because he might have a family that would miss him."

"She's right," Kaylee agreed, blinking rapidly to stop her tears from falling. She was sick and tired of crying, especially when she had so much to be happy about. "They would miss him."

"Why don't you two go watch some cartoons?" Ava suggested. "We'll have dinner in a little while."

"Yes!" Colt yelled, raising his arms in triumph before zipping up the stairs. Brianna was right behind him. "Excellent."

"We don't let them watch a lot of television," Logan explained with a chuckle. "So they're excited."

Ava sighed and sat down on the couch. "Let me amend my husband's statement. We try to not let them watch too much television. Sometimes we're exhausted parents and it happens."

Reed sat down on the ottoman next to Kaylee, her hand still in his. It felt safe and warm and she never wanted to be without this man. She loved him so much. As happened so often, she was captured by his good looks. Her gaze wandered over his wide shoulders, his strong chin, and square jaw. His dark hair, shot with gray, badly needed a trim and the wind outside had tousled it a little. And those hazel eyes. Soft and full of love.

Shit, they were looking at her right now. She'd been totally busted staring at him.

From the smile on his face, he didn't seem to mind.

Kaylee dragged her attention from her amazing husband back to Ava. "Should we tell them our news now?"

"I think we should."

Logan and Reed were both frowning, glancing back and forth between their wives, clearly perplexed.

"I have to say that I'm curious," Reed said. "We're had a great deal of news lately."

They certainly had. Four days into Kaylee's recovery, Reed had received a phone call from the town council that employed him as sheriff.

He was fired.

The new mayor had taken office and fired the entire law enforcement staff, Reed and all of his deputies, and installed his own people. Small town politics could be cutthroat. Reed would be paid out a severance as required by his contract, plus all of his accrued vacation and sick time. He would have plenty of time to find another job.

"Ava and I are going to write a book together. A series of books, actually," Kaylee announced with a grin. She was excited about the future. She and Reed had talked about finding new dreams and this was one of them. "True crime, specifically cold cases."

Logan's brow arched as his gaze bounced between his wife and Kaylee. "You're going to write about it or you're going to try and solve the cases?"

Ava shrugged. "Maybe a little bit of both."

"This might be time for my news then," Logan said, rubbing his chin. "Jason is staring a new division of the consulting firm and I'm going to head it up."

Ava squealed and wrapped him in a hug. "That's wonderful. Wait…this is a desk job, right? You're not going back into the field, are you?"

"This is a desk job," Logan confirmed, dropping a kiss on her lips. "But I need a second in command to help me."

Logan looked at Reed whose face was turning red. "What Logan is trying to say is that he's asked me to join the consulting firm. Work with him in this new division, building it from the ground up. And yes, it's a desk job. Before you say anything, I haven't made a decision. I wanted to talk to you about it, baby."

Kaylee searched her husband's expression for a clue as to how he felt, what he wanted. Damn his poker face. He wasn't giving anything away.

"What do you want to do?" she finally asked. He needed new dreams, too.

"I think," he replied slowly. "That I'd like to do it, but we need to talk about this. It would mean selling our house, moving here to be closer to the office. It might mean some long days and weekends getting things going. We need to build a brand-new team of people."

Ava was practically jumping up and down on the couch at the news. Kaylee wasn't exactly against the idea of being closer to her best friend and she wasn't feeling all that kindly about a town that had just summarily dismissed her husband. Jobs weren't easy to find there either, so moving had probably been a foregone conclusion.

"Say yes, say yes," Ava chanted, a gigantic grin on her face. "Please say yes."

Kaylee reached over and placed both her hands in his, their gazes locked. "If this is what you want to do, then I'm in complete support."

"Yes!"

For a moment, Ava looked exactly like Colt when he had permission to watch cartoons out of the blue.

"Ava and Kaylee, together again," Logan laughed. "Someone

needs to alert the media. This might be dangerous."

"Hey, watch what you're saying about my sister." Ava elbowed her husband playfully. "You and Reed together could be just as crazy."

Sister. Yes, Ava was the sister that Kaylee had never had.

Shit, I'm going to cry again. Someone make it stop. I'm just so darn grateful. This almost didn't happen.

"What can you tell us about this new division?" Ava asked much later. They'd finished dinner, cleaned up the dishes, put the twins to bed, and were now relaxing with full bellies. Actually, she'd just watched most of that from her perch on the recliner whle the others bustled around her. Kaylee made a mental note to send an effusive thank you card to Jason and Brinley. The food had been fantastic and it was even better that Ava didn't have to spend all evening in the kitchen preparing it. "What sort of consulting will you be doing?"

Reed and Logan exchanged a quick glance that immediately had Kaylee's attention.

"Did I ask a loaded question?"

Because it sure looked like it.

"We're going to run the serials and stalkers division," Reed finally answered. "You could say that Logan and I have some expertise there."

They certainly did. More than most.

"Serials and stalkers," Ava repeated, nodding her head. "That sounds right up your alley. Maybe you'll get a few cold cases and we can write about them."

Logan was already shaking his head and looking damn worried. "Absolutely not, woman. You – both of you – are not ever going to be in danger again. I'm putting my foot down about this. The man of the house has spoken."

Kaylee had to press the pillow to her stomach because laughing still hurt a little. Reed hadn't said anything but he looked just as concerned as Logan, maybe more.

"We wouldn't dream of getting in the middle of your investigation," Kaylee assured them. "We'd just write about it. Right, Ava?"

"Right," her friend agreed. "Completely out of the line of fire. We're going to keep to being authors."

Logan groaned and scraped his hand down his face. "Do you believe them?"

"Nope," Reed replied, rubbing at his temple where a headache was surely blooming. "Not a word."

Leaning over, Kaylee pressed a kiss to his stubbly cheek. "New dreams, remember?"

"New dreams," he agreed, turning so he could whisper in her ear. His words only for her. "But let's keep them non-lethal. I want the most exciting thing we do to be in the bedroom."

He was far too modest. A lifetime with Reed wasn't going to be boring in the least. But if it did get a little mundane, they knew what to do.

Get new dreams.

I hope you enjoyed revisiting Reed, Kaylee, Logan and Ava! There's much more to come in the Cowboy Justice Association World. Thank you for reading Seeking Justice!

Don't miss a thing! Sign up to be notified of Olivia's new releases:

oliviajaymesoptin.instapage.com

About the Author

Olivia Jaymes is a wife, mother, lover of sexy romance, and caffeine addict. She lives with her husband and son in central Florida and spends her days with handsome alpha males and spunky heroines.

She is currently working on a new contemporary romance series – ManTrap – in addition to the ongoing Danger Incorporated series and the Cowboy Justice Association series.

Visit Olivia Jaymes at
www.OliviaJaymes.com

Other Titles by Olivia Jaymes

Danger Incorporated

Damsel In Danger
Hiding From Danger
Discarded Heart Novella
Indecent Danger
Embracing Danger
Danger In The Night
Reunited With Danger
Window to Danger
Road to Danger
Unwanted Danger

Cowboy Justice Association

Cowboy Command
Justice Healed
Cowboy Truth
Cowboy Famous
Cowboy Cool
Imperfect Justice
The Deputies
Justice Inked
Justice Reborn
Vengeful Justice
Justice Divided

Military Moguls

Champagne and Bullets
Diamonds and Revolvers
Caviar and Covert Ops
Emeralds, Rubies, and Camouflage

Midnight Blue Beach

Wicked After Midnight
Midnight Of No Return
Kiss Midnight Goodbye

The Hollywood Showmance Chronicles

A Kiss For the Cameras
Swinging From A Star
Wild on the Red Carpet
Love in the Spotlight
And the Winner is

Made in the USA
Columbia, SC
10 January 2025

51569646R00129